A Particular Attachment

A Particular Attachment

GERALDINE TAYLOR

Copyright © 2025 Geraldine Taylor

The moral right of the author has been asserted.

Apart from any fair dealing for the purposes of research or private study, or criticism or review, as permitted under the Copyright, Designs and Patents Act 1988, this publication may only be reproduced, stored or transmitted, in any form or by any means, with the prior permission in writing of the publishers, or in the case of reprographic reproduction in accordance with the terms of licences issued by the Copyright Licensing Agency. Enquiries concerning reproduction outside those terms should be sent to the publishers.

The manufacturer's authorised representative in the EU for product safety is Authorised Rep Compliance Ltd, 71 Lower Baggot Street, Dublin D02 P593 Ireland
(www.arccompliance.com)

This is a work of fiction. Names, characters, businesses, places, events and incidents are either the products of the author's imagination or used in a fictitious manner. Any resemblance to actual persons, living or dead, or actual events is purely coincidental.

Troubador Publishing Ltd
Unit E2 Airfield Business Park,
Harrison Road, Market Harborough,
Leicestershire LE16 7UL
Tel: 0116 279 2299
Email: books@troubador.co.uk
Web: www.troubador.co.uk

ISBN 9781836281849

British Library Cataloguing in Publication Data.
A catalogue record for this book is available from the British Library.

Printed and bound in Great Britain by 4edge Limited
Typeset in 11pt Minion Pro by Troubador Publishing Ltd, Leicester, UK

For Christina, Caroline and Christine

1

Heather Delaney stood by the open window. Her consulting room overlooked a leafy square, and between clients, she liked to watch the birds in the trees and the people sitting on benches around the grass. Usually, it helped to clear, or at least settle, her mind before having to pay complete attention to someone else. This afternoon, her mind would not settle. She was just waiting, hoping the phone would ring, because her last client of the day, Phoebe, hadn't turned up. This was the second week in a row that she hadn't attended, and Heather hadn't heard from her.

She tried sitting at her desk but found it impossible to focus on any of the tasks she might have got on with – client notes, reports, responding to emails. She would rather Phoebe came to the appointments, drunk or sober, because now she was worried.

Phoebe didn't call. Heather went to the small kitchen in the corridor to refill her glass with water and returned to her room. She'd sent Phoebe a text the week before when she'd missed her appointment, but there had been no response. Could she be acting out because they were coming to the end of the course of therapy? Heather didn't think so. She had a feeling something was wrong.

At five fifteen, she decided to go against protocol and called Phoebe's mobile number.

She was surprised when a woman answered and said, 'Hello. Police. Hold on, please.'

Heather thought the woman had a Geordie accent. She could hear voices in the background, and then a man came on the line.

'This is Detective Inspector John Kelly. Who's speaking, please?' His voice was mellow, pleasant.

'My name is Heather Delaney. I was hoping to speak to Phoebe, Phoebe Summers.' She wondered if this man really was a policeman.

'Are you a friend of Phoebe Summers?'

'I'm a psychotherapist. Phoebe didn't attend her appointment this afternoon. Is she all right?'

'I'm afraid not, Ms Delaney. I'm sorry to have to tell you that Phoebe has had an accident.'

'What kind of accident? Is she in hospital?' Phoebe didn't drive. Did she have a bicycle? Maybe she'd been run over.

'It was an accident at home. We've informed the next of kin so I can tell you that she died as a result of her injuries.'

Heather leant forward so her forearms were on the desk, her phone slipped between her fingers. She closed her eyes; she felt sick, and her head was strangely empty.

'Ms Delaney…'

Heather sat upright and brought the phone to her ear. 'Yes?'

'How long have you known Phoebe?'

'She's been coming to see me for ten weeks.'

'We'd like to talk to you,' said DI Kelly. 'As someone who knew Phoebe well, you may be able to help us.'

'Of course. What kind of accident was it?'

'I'm sorry, I can't say any more at this stage.'

'Was anyone else involved?'

'At the moment we don't know. We're still investigating. As I say, we'd like to come and see you, as soon as possible, maybe you can help us understand what happened.'

After arranging to meet the police the following day, Heather called the manager of the therapy centre, Vicki Hammond. She was still in her office and Heather asked if she could come and see her straight away. Vicki said she was preparing to leave and was it important. Heather said it was, put down the phone and set off along the corridor to Vicki's room.

Vicki was standing behind her large desk, pulling on a cream linen jacket.

'I'm sorry to call you at this time of the day,' said Heather. 'I've just had some shocking news.'

Vicki indicated a chair with wooden arms facing the desk.

Heather sat on the edge of the chair. 'One of my clients has died,' she said. 'Phoebe Summers.' She felt a catch in her voice and cleared her throat. 'The police said Phoebe had an accident at home and she's dead. They wouldn't give me any more details.'

Vicki's eyes widened almost imperceptibly and then her face settled into an efficient yet concerned expression. She hung her jacket on the back of her chair and sat down.

'Did the police call you?' she asked.

'Phoebe was due to come and see me at four o'clock and she didn't attend. She didn't come last week either, so I called her mobile. The police had it and they answered. They're coming to interview me here tomorrow. I thought I should let you know.'

Heather had no desire to talk to Vicki about Phoebe. She wanted to cry and was desperate to keep this conversation as brief as possible.

Vicki pushed a box of tissues across the desk; Heather took one and put it in her trouser pocket.

'You've done the right thing coming to me before talking to the police,' said Vicki. 'Depending on how she died, they might ask you… Did you think she might…? Did Phoebe tell you she had suicidal thoughts?'

'No. She was depressed when she started therapy and sometimes said she wished she wasn't here. But the last time I saw her she was upbeat, positive; her mood was improved.'

She knew Vicki was wondering if she might have missed suicidal thoughts or intentions in her sessions with Phoebe. Vicki was concerned about liability, bad publicity.

'Do they suspect suicide?' asked Vicki.

'I don't think so,' said Heather. 'I don't think she would have killed herself. I shall tell them that.'

Vicki nodded. 'Of course, as you know, the duty of confidentiality extends after death.'

'But an exception can be made in the case of a serious crime, I believe,' said Heather.

Vicki's eyes widened again. 'Do the police suspect a crime has been committed here?'

'I don't know,' said Heather.

'Do you think a crime has been committed?' asked Vicki.

Heather hesitated, and then she said, 'It's possible. Until they tell me more, I don't know.'

'Ah! You need to tread carefully in that case,' said Vicki, and she turned to reach for her jacket. 'Now go home, do some yoga or whatever will help, and mull things over. If you want to talk, at any time, I'm here.'

Heather left Vicki's office. She sighed as she closed the door. Vicki was the last person she would choose to talk things over with, but she had to be informed of what was happening.

Heather went home by bus and tube. She'd managed to buy a house in Chiswick when prices were low and she'd inherited money from her aunt. She was grateful to have it and felt lucky when she thought about how much house prices had increased in London since then.

Years ago, in another life, after a difficult day she would have gone to a pub on the way home; she would either have phoned a friend to meet her or gone on her own. She was used to haunting bars alone back then. There was something freeing about it, to walk in alone, in smart work clothes, with an expensive work bag, and sit at the bar, order a glass of white wine, light a cigarette, chat up the barman or barmaid. She would often be approached by some man, usually a creep who fancied himself, who would offer her a drink, make bad jokes, and she would order another drink, maybe a bottle, and retreat to a table.

On one occasion she'd left her bag at the bar and the creep had brought it over to her. She'd thanked him, said she was expecting someone. Alone at the table, she would go over the trying or distressing events and encounters of the day until, after a few glasses of wine, they dissolved into reverie or bonhomie, and she could go home. A couple of times she was approached at the bar or the table by a man she found attractive and amusing, and she would let him buy her a drink and she might leave with him.

Now, sitting on the tube, she felt her face grow hot at the memory. She took out her phone to distract herself.

When she got home, she took her shoes off in the hall and went into the living room. The back part of the room, the dining area, contained a large table that she used as a desk. At the therapy centre she kept her desk clear. Her table at home was covered with piles of papers, files and journals and she liked it that way; she knew exactly what was there and could find whatever she needed almost straight away. If she wanted to use her laptop on the table, she would move a couple of piles on to the floor. The laptop usually lived on the glass-topped coffee table in the front, lounge area of the room, within easy reach of her armchair. She still had the leather work bag, though it was well worn now. She put it on a chair and walked through to the kitchen to put the kettle on. She wasn't hungry, felt all churned up, but she would eat something light later on, watch some television and try to take her mind off what had happened to Phoebe.

She woke early the next morning, feeling anxious. Thinking she ought to look smart for the police interview, she put on a midi-length patterned skirt, a black top and black sandals. Her dark-brown hair had been cut recently into a neat bob. The hairdresser had pointed out some grey and suggested highlights. Maybe next time, she'd said. She stood before her full-length mirror and decided she looked OK, although when she stood sideways on, she saw that she could do with losing a few pounds again; she would have to make time for swimming or running.

She was pleased she had two clients to see that morning; they gave her something to focus on. At ten o'clock she saw David. He was overweight and had a history of binge eating. He'd lived with his mother until the age of thirty-nine, when he married a woman he met at work. He was having a stressful time at work now and had started bingeing again. He'd told his wife about his problems and she had seemed to accept him, but the reality had shocked her. He was on a waiting list for bariatric surgery and wanted to examine why he behaved as he did and try to make changes.

Her eleven o'clock was Rosemary, a slight woman in her early seventies with curly white hair who dressed like a hippy student in jeans, cheesecloth smocks and sandals, and rode a bicycle with a basket on the front. She appeared whimsical and carefree but was so eager to please that she found it difficult to make decisions and to live her life. Each week she would come in smiling tentatively and say, in a childlike voice, 'Am I late? Sorry.' Her husband had died eight years earlier and she still sought to please him, and anyone else she had dealings with.

Heather said goodbye to Rosemary at eleven fifty. The police were due at twelve. Right on cue, she had a call from reception telling her they'd arrived, so she went downstairs. DI Kelly and a female colleague were standing by the reception desk. He came forward, introduced himself and shook her hand. He was dark, medium height, about fifty. He hadn't shaved recently. His colleague, a blonde woman in a navy trouser suit, introduced herself as DS Yvonne Simmonds. She had a Geordie accent, so Heather assumed this was the woman she'd spoken to on the phone the day before.

Heather took them up to her room and offered tea, which they declined. She invited them to sit in the two armchairs in the counselling area of the room near the window and pulled up a hard chair for herself. DS Simmonds took the hard chair from her and indicated one of the armchairs, so Heather sat almost opposite DI Kelly, at that slight angle used by therapists with clients to avoid a feeling of confrontation. She thought about police interviews she'd seen in crime dramas on television, where one or two officers sat directly facing the suspect across a table, maybe with a lawyer next to the suspect, for protection.

'Thank you for seeing us so quickly, Ms Delaney,' said DI Kelly.

'I want to be of assistance, if I can.'

He nodded. 'When did you last see Phoebe Summers?'

'Two weeks ago, Wednesday, here at the centre.'

'How long have you known her, did you say?'

'She started coming to see me in May this year. I've been seeing her once a week – well, most weeks. What happened to her?'

'First, what can you tell us about her?' asked DI Kelly.

The DS sat, ankles crossed, with a pen poised over her

notebook. DI Kelly didn't cross his legs, he sat with his feet firmly planted, yet there was a nerviness about him. *He looks tired*, Heather thought.

'What do you want to know?' she asked.

'Why did she need a therapist?'

Heather wanted to say that many people who were functioning well attended therapy to understand themselves better or to resolve certain issues. It wasn't that a few people were so messed up they needed therapy and everyone else didn't. She suppressed her irritation.

'She was anxious. Things that happened to her in the past made her vulnerable in some ways. Her father died when she was fourteen and she didn't get on with her mother. She got involved in relationships that weren't good for her.'

The DI leant forward slightly. 'What do you mean?'

'Relationships with controlling and abusive men. Her most recent boyfriend was like that. But she'd freed herself from him, as far as I know.'

'Was his name Martin?'

'Yes.'

'We're aware of him. Would you say Phoebe was depressed?'

'When I first started seeing her, yes.'

'Did she ever express suicidal thoughts?'

'She said she didn't want to be here a couple of times, but that was at the beginning of therapy, and she never expressed suicidal intentions.'

'She didn't want to be here. What did you take that to mean?'

'She felt she'd had enough,' Heather took a deep

breath, 'I suppose of struggling with anxiety, things going badly, feeling bad about herself.'

'Was she depressed when you last saw her?'

'No, she wasn't. She was positive, optimistic. Why are you asking? What happened to her?'

'Phoebe fell from the balcony of her flat.'

Heather's mind went blank with shock. She brought her hands together into a praying position and then returned them to rest on her knees. She closed her eyes for a few seconds and then looked straight at DI Kelly.

'When was this?' she asked him.

'Last week, Monday night.'

'I sent her a text last Wednesday, when she didn't attend her appointment. Did you see it?'

'Yes,' he said. 'I apologise. We would have been in touch with you in due course. Do you think it's possible that Phoebe jumped deliberately, that she took her own life?'

'Definitely not, Detective Inspector.' Heather was aware of DI Kelly's brown eyes looking intently back at her. 'Was anyone else there when this happened?'

'There's no evidence that anyone else was in the flat at the time of the accident.'

DS Simmonds spoke now. 'Did Phoebe drink to excess?'

'Why do you ask?'

'From evidence at the scene, it's clear she'd been drinking,' said DI Kelly. 'We're awaiting a toxicology report. It's possible that she simply fell. She was very drunk, and she fell, maybe she was leaning over the balcony, lost her balance.'

'She'd cut down her drinking recently,' said Heather. 'I suppose it's possible. Do you really think that's what happened? How likely is it?'

'I can't say at the moment,' said DI Kelly. He stood up and DS Simmonds closed her notebook and stood up too. 'Thank you, Ms Delaney,' said DI Kelly. 'This is obviously disturbing for you. Were you fond of Phoebe?'

Heather got to her feet. She didn't want him looking down at her. 'She was my client.'

'You must form an attachment sometimes.'

'My job would be very difficult if I became attached to my clients,' said Heather. 'This is such a tragic waste of a young life, and I hope you find out what happened to her.'

When she'd shown the officers out, she reflected that in her drinking days, at a time like this she wouldn't just have gone to a bar after work for a few glasses of wine, she would have gone home and hit the vodka.

She went out to get some lunch. Today she would sit in a café, not take a sandwich back to the office. She wanted to be on neutral ground, to think. She ordered an Americano with cold milk on the side. The barista would bring her tuna panini over to her table. She liked the familiar pinkish walls of this coffee bar chain, the sepia photos of Italian scenes, the nostalgic music in the background – Van Morrison, Stevie Wonder.

She found herself thinking about Phoebe's most recent boyfriend, Martin, about how he was very possessive and had been physically abusive. She wondered if he'd had anything to do with Phoebe's death. They said there was no evidence that anyone else was in the flat. Perhaps, as the investigation progressed, evidence would come to light.

2

Heather left it a week and called DI John Kelly for an update. He told her an autopsy had been performed to establish cause of death and the coroner had issued a cremation certificate so the funeral could go ahead.

'What was the cause of death?' she asked him.

'She had multiple injuries,' he said.

Heather flinched. 'What injuries?'

'We'll have to wait for the inquest hearing for the full picture,' said DI Kelly. 'You'll be able to attend, if you want to.'

'When will that be?' asked Heather.

'When the coroner has completed his investigation.'

She sighed. 'And your investigation? That will continue, I assume.'

'It's not a suspicious death, so no, the coroner will investigate.'

Both were silent on the line for a moment. Heather felt impatient, frustrated, but what could she do?

'I'd like to go to the funeral,' she said. 'Will you let me know when it is?'

She had leave booked in August but didn't arrange to go away anywhere. She bought Lycra crops, vests and running shoes, and ran in the grounds of Chiswick House. Sometimes, when running or walking, she would start off mulling over a work issue, such as what to make of what a client had said or who she wanted to discuss in supervision. Or she might be thinking about contacting a friend to arrange something for the weekend, maybe a trip to a gallery or lunch or drinks. She thought of evening drinks less often than she used to, as she enjoyed being in pubs less, and for shorter periods, since she'd stopped drinking alcohol. Whatever she was thinking about, her thoughts always came back to Phoebe. Her supervisor at the therapy centre was skilled and insightful, but Heather couldn't share with her what she was thinking and feeling about Phoebe. She couldn't tell her supervisor that she wanted to conduct her own investigation into Phoebe's death.

Heather arrived at the crematorium in a taxi, just before the service was due to start. It was a bright September day; the leaves were turning yellow and brown, and daisies and cyclamens were blooming in well-tended beds. She could hear that inside the chapel the organist was playing "Jesu, Joy of Man's Desiring". She entered the chapel and slid into an empty pew, on the left, just behind the other mourners. She picked up the order of service booklet from the pew and sat down. It gave her a shock, seeing the photographs of Phoebe in the booklet. She would look at them later. The coffin, on a stand at the front, was adorned with a bouquet of traditional white lilies and the heavy, sickly perfume from them filled Heather's nostrils. She reminded herself to specify that she did not want white lilies at her funeral – flowers, yes, but not funereal lilies.

There were twenty or so mourners. A middle-aged woman with short blonde hair sat at the front to the right of the aisle, next to an older woman; *they could be Phoebe's mother and grandmother*, Heather thought. Most of the older people had opted to wear traditional black. The younger ones, who looked to be in their thirties, were dressed in more everyday clothes, the young men in jeans and jackets, the young women in trousers, or long skirts, and colourful scarves.

The minister, fortyish with receding hair, stepped up to the lectern and the music stopped. He welcomed everyone and invited them to stand and sing "All Things Bright and Beautiful". The singing was thin and patchy, carried by a couple of confident singers, a tenor and a soprano, who were standing together near the front.

They all took their seats again and the minister talked about Phoebe losing her father when she was fourteen and her mother bringing her up alone. She did well at school and went to university in London, where she got her degree in English literature. She had then studied for a teaching English qualification and taught English to foreign students. She'd recently started working for a mental health charity. The minister turned to look over at Phoebe's mother and grandmother and said what an untimely and shocking death it had been, such a tragedy for her family.

He invited one of her friends to come up and say a few words. Heather saw Phoebe's mother take a deep breath and look up at the young woman mounting the rostrum.

Sarah had long black hair and brown eyes lined with kohl. She wore a knee-length red and gold jacket over black top and trousers. She began in a wavering voice, but her delivery grew stronger as she spoke. Phoebe wrote wonderful poetry, she said. That was how they had met. They performed together at open mic events.

At that moment, there was a noise at the back of the chapel, the sound of the door closing. Sarah's expression of rapt concentration changed to one of dismay and irritation. Heather turned, along with other mourners, to see that a young man had entered and was taking a seat at the back. He was dark, with hair curling over his collar and striking green eyes that were red-rimmed, as if from weeping.

Heather's heart began to beat fast, and her hands were shaking. She tightened her grip on the order of service. Could that be Martin?

Sarah cleared her throat. 'So, I've written this poem for Phoebe.'

Her delivery was faultless, her voice rising and falling. The poem told how she thought of her friend all the time, dreamt of her and looked for her in cafés and bars they used to go to together. In the last verse she compared Phoebe to the moon, saying, '*Like the moon, you were bright and shining.*'

Sarah returned to her seat and was hugged by the friends sitting on either side of her. The minister did a reading about God's many mansions and said the Lord's Prayer and the committal, and the coffin rolled away through the curtains. Phoebe's mother swayed slightly, and a low moan was heard – Heather thought it was the grandmother. Some of the friends were crying. Heather looked down at her own clasped hands; she wanted to keep her emotions under control. They sang the final hymn, "Abide with Me", and then Phoebe's mother led the way up the aisle, her own mother holding onto her arm. The old lady looked grief-stricken, the mother stoical.

Outside, along the chapel wall, floral tributes were displayed, and there were several bouquets and a wreath for Phoebe. Heather looked at the cards on them: Mum, Nan, Auntie and Uncle, Sarah and other friends. Nothing from Martin.

Heather was keen to talk to the young man who had arrived late. She looked around and saw him hanging back behind the others, lighting a cigarette. She started towards him but felt a hand on her arm.

'I don't think we've met. I'm Jean, Phoebe's mother.'

'Heather. I'm so sorry for your loss. I worked with Phoebe. I hope you don't mind me coming.'

'Not at all. Where was she working?'

'The local Mind organisation. Phoebe worked there in the housing team. It was only for a matter of weeks, sadly.'

'I didn't know,' said Jean. 'We hadn't been in touch for some time. Did she tell you?' She grimaced. 'I don't suppose she had a good word to say about me.'

'That's not the case,' said Heather. 'Phoebe loved you; you can be sure of that.'

'Thank you,' said Jean. 'You must come back to the house. It's in Farnham.'

'Maybe for a short time, I have to catch a train,' said Heather. 'Can I ask, who is that young man over there?'

'I don't know. I wonder who he can be. Phoebe had a lot of friends in London I didn't know.'

'Will you excuse me?' said Heather.

At that moment, a woman came up wanting to talk to Jean, and Heather walked over to join the young man by the fence.

'I don't suppose you have a spare one of those, do you?'

He took out his packet of cigarettes. Heather took one and he lit it with a disposable lighter. She could smell beer on his breath; the red-rimmed eyes may not have been from weeping. He was good-looking, tall and slim. Under his black jacket, he had on a blue T-shirt and jeans. The jacket was in need of dry-cleaning and he had a slightly seedy, in-need-of-looking-after air about him.

'Thank you,' she said. 'I'm Heather. May I ask your name?'

'Martin,' he said.

Heather's heart began to beat fast again. She took a deep draw on the cigarette and felt a bit light-headed; she hadn't smoked in a while.

'I needed that,' she said. 'Are you going back to the house?'

'I reckon not,' he said. 'I'm somewhat persona non grata.'

'Oh, are you?'

'It's a long story. I don't get on with some of Phoebe's friends.'

'Really?'

'Yeah.' He didn't offer any further elaboration.

'How did you know Phoebe?' she asked.

'She was my girlfriend,' he said. He looked into Heather's face as if challenging her to argue. And then his green eyes were full of tears. 'What do I do now she's gone?'

'If you want to talk, I'm a good listener,' said Heather.

He shrugged.

'Where do you live?' she asked.

'London, Shepherd's Bush.'

'I live not far from there,' said Heather. 'If you give me your number, I'll call you. We can meet up, talk about Phoebe.'

A man was holding the bathroom door open for her, so Heather thanked him and went in. The bathroom had a sloping ceiling, white fittings and turquoise curtains, towels and liquid soap. *God, tights are uncomfortable*, she thought, as she manoeuvred them down so she could take a pee. It was also uncomfortable being there, at the funeral and now the wake. She'd been unsure whether to come to the house, but Jean had arranged for someone to give her a lift and curiosity had got the better of her. Martin was not invited and had left; she had turned around and he was gone. The couple who brought her to the house had expressed the view that it was going to the big city that had been the beginning of the end for Phoebe. Heather couldn't linger in the bathroom because people were waiting to use it, so she washed her hands, checked her clothes, glanced in the mirror and went downstairs.

She'd been hoping for a milling-about situation in which she could move around discreetly, but how could it be like that when there were so few mourners? The people who had arrived so far were sitting around the lounge, drinking tea and talking about their journeys, the weather. Heather took a cup of tea proffered by Phoebe's grandmother.

'What will they do with her flowers, Jean?' Heather heard the grandmother ask.

Then the young people arrived, and the gathering became noisier and more informal; people got to their feet, started to help themselves to sandwiches and stood around in pairs and small groups.

Heather put two sandwiches and a samosa on a plate and went over to where Sarah was standing near the French window with one of the young men.

'Sarah, I'm Heather,' she said, and Sarah turned to her. 'I enjoyed your tribute very much. Phoebe's mother must be so pleased you're here.'

The young man waved to someone, excused himself and moved away.

'Phoebe was like one of my best mates.' Sarah's brown eyes were large and sad, her lashes thick with mascara. 'Are you a friend of the family?'

'I worked with Phoebe,' said Heather. 'You must have been very shocked when you heard she was dead.'

'God, yes, it was a huge shock,' said Sarah, 'but in a way, I wasn't surprised, you know?'

'Why do you say that?'

'Well, there was something tragic about her. She had these mood swings. She liked drama. I guess it was because of losing her dad when she was young, not getting on with her stepdad, I don't know.'

'The stepdad, he's not here, is he?' Heather looked around the room.

'Alan's not been on the scene for a while,' said Sarah.

'Ah, yes, Alan. I've never met him.'

'Me neither.'

'The young man that came into the chapel late, do you know him?'

'Martin? Unfortunately, yes.'

'He told me Phoebe was his girlfriend,' said Heather. 'He seemed really upset.'

'Phoebe finished with him weeks ago, but he kept calling her, texting, going round to her flat. He couldn't accept it.'

'Oh dear,' said Heather.

'He was really controlling, and he hit her, more than once. She had a split lip one night and she admitted he'd done it. He got jealous. And when they were going out, Phoebe never even looked at another man. He's a maniac. How did you know Phoebe, did you say?'

'I worked with her. At the mental health charity,' said Heather.

'Ah, I see. What do the police think happened to her, do you know?'

'They think it was an accident or suicide,' said Heather. 'They've left it to the coroner to investigate.'

'So they can't be bothered,' said Sarah.

'You don't think she killed herself?'

'No way. She'd been out with this really cool guy at the weekend and she was due to see him again later in the week.'

'Ah! I didn't know that.' *Thank you, Sarah*, she thought.

On the way home in the train, Heather looked at the order of service booklet. The photo on the front showed Phoebe as a young woman, smiling, pretty, with her honey-blonde hair and blue eyes. She looked so alive and happy. Inside the booklet were photos of her as a baby and a toddler and as a child of about five in a swimsuit on a beach. There was one of her as a schoolgirl in uniform – Phoebe had a knowing smile, half smart, half shy. Another showed her cuddling a kitten. There were more photos of her in her early years than as an adult. Heather felt numb looking at those childhood photos, reluctant to contemplate how Phoebe's mother and grandmother must be feeling. She turned again to the photo on the front; that was how she wanted to hold Phoebe in her mind, how she wanted to remember her.

3

Heather worked at the therapy centre on Tuesdays, Wednesdays and Thursdays. On Mondays and Fridays, she went to a consulting room she rented in a street of terraced houses in Hammersmith. The back room on the ground floor of the house was the consulting room and the front room served as a waiting room. She referred to it as Number 27.

She had some time between clients for thinking and writing, and usually found the room a good place for writing – she'd published a couple of articles and had ideas for papers she wanted to write, and a possible book. She was there today, but although she could focus when she had a client in front of her, lately her concentration was not very good when it came to writing. She was easily distracted and preoccupied with what had happened to Phoebe.

She leant back in her swivel chair and looked up at the Monet calendar pinned above her desk, without really seeing it. She recalled the detective inspector asking her if she was fond of Phoebe and her terse reply that she was a client, her denial of any attachment. In fact, she'd known she was at risk of losing her therapeutic distance, of getting too involved. Now, when she was not with a client, she found herself thinking about Phoebe, and the only explanation she could come up with for her preoccupation was that she had experienced similar issues to Phoebe – a stepfather, a difficult relationship with her mother, anxiety, drinking to excess, toxic relationships. She identified with her.

She had handwritten notes from their sessions together and now she carried the notes with her in a plastic folder in her work bag. As she didn't have another client until later that day, she pushed aside the papers on her desk, reached into her bag and took out the notes. She began to read them again, from the beginning. She wanted to review Phoebe's story and the people who had played a part in it.

Phoebe had been experiencing anxiety and depression and had been referred for a course of therapy by her GP. She was drinking a lot when Heather first started seeing her but had reduced her alcohol intake as the sessions went on. She seemed relieved to be able to open up and it had been relatively easy to build a rapport with her.

She talked a great deal about her boyfriend Martin, saying he'd had a difficult childhood but was a fantastic musician and artist. She and Martin had been happy together at first and he used to spend a lot of time in her flat. She was teaching English to foreign students and when she sent him away so she could prepare her lessons, he looked abandoned and miserable; he had no job and was signing on. The relationship deteriorated after the first heady days, as he became jealous and possessive and assaulted her on more than one occasion. She said she knew she should end the relationship, but she was in love with him.

Phoebe was successful in getting a job with a mental health charity and Martin got her into trouble there by constantly phoning her at work; he would complain that she had no time for him and accuse her of seeing other men. She was unable to be firm about not taking his calls because she was afraid he might harm himself – he'd said he didn't want to live without her. Her manager had intervened with a formal warning. Phoebe agreed to turn off her mobile at work and the manager asked the receptionist not to put his calls through. Phoebe was very upset about this trouble at work but was still unwilling to break off with him. She was needy herself and said that his neediness made her feel like the strong one. Some weeks into the therapy, things with Martin took an even darker turn. One day, a young woman stopped Phoebe as she walked home from work and said she thought a man was following her, that he'd been dodging behind cars and hedges. It turned out to be Martin. Heather had expressed alarm at this behaviour, and it had been the final straw for Phoebe – she finished with him soon afterwards.

Heather had written warnings for herself in the session notes because she'd become aware that there were parallels with her own past issues, which made it difficult for her to be objective, and she knew she needed to reflect on that and keep it in her mind.

Phoebe's father had died when she was fourteen and her mother had remarried two years later. She found it difficult that her mother had brought this other man, Alan, into their home, but she planned to go to university and told herself it was good that her mother had someone. Alan was very different from her father, who had been a journalist and an avid reader. Alan was a builder, useful around the house, and he made her mother laugh. By all accounts he did his best with Phoebe, including helping her with money when she was at university. Heather had wondered if there was something Phoebe was not telling her about Alan, but nothing of concern had come to light in the sessions. He had acquitted himself well when Phoebe had thrown herself at him on one occasion when she was in her twenties. She said she'd been assaulted by a boyfriend and had a black eye, and Heather had noted that she'd had more than one abusive relationship. She'd gone home to her mother's, and Alan had wanted to go to London and sort out this boyfriend. Phoebe wanted him to fight for her and resented her mother for putting a stop to it. Later, when drunk, she'd sat on Alan's knee, and he'd pushed her off and told her to go to bed. Heather had noted her own mixed feelings about his response: she was relieved, but also disappointed – which shocked her at the time – and she supposed that was because inappropriate behaviour on the part of the stepfather might have been a factor contributing to low mood and anxiety, something they could have addressed. Phoebe had insisted that the episode had blown over and she got on fine with Alan. They hadn't discussed it again in the sessions. Alan had visited her in London since then, and he'd been supportive.

Phoebe had gained in confidence as the therapy

progressed. She'd been shaken and set back by Martin's disturbing and controlling behaviour, but once she had finished with him, she'd begun to thrive. They had started to talk about whether to bring the therapy to an end after twelve weeks, or whether Phoebe could benefit from a further course, and then she had failed to attend for two weeks, and then... the terrible news.

Heather wasn't entirely satisfied that Alan was above suspicion; in a way, he was too good to be true. But it was Martin she kept coming back to. She knew he had continued to call and text Phoebe, and turn up at her flat, after she'd finished with him. Heather was sure that the police should still be investigating Phoebe's death and that Martin should be a person of interest to them.

She put the notes in her bag and stood up to stretch her back. She wanted to talk things over with someone, and she knew just the person she wanted as a sounding board. She picked up her phone.

Years before, she had worked briefly for a private investigation outfit. It was an admin role but had given her a taste for investigation. She'd decided to pursue a career in which she would investigate the workings of the mind in a consulting room, but she'd stayed in contact with Max Gallagher.

Max was already in the pub when Heather arrived. He was sitting at a table opposite the bar reading a newspaper, with a pint of Guinness in front of him and a plastic nicotine inhalator between his stained fingers. He was unshaven and his wavy grey hair needed cutting.

When he saw Heather, he started to get up. She

gestured to him to sit back down and went to the bar to order a coffee. She returned and sat opposite Max.

'Straightened them all out, have you?' asked Max.

'If only,' said Heather. 'But then I'd be out of a job, wouldn't I?' She saw that he was reading the obituaries page. 'Anyone you know?' she asked.

'No, but I like to see who's popped off before me.'

A barman brought over a cafetière on a tray with a cup and saucer, jug of milk and a bowl of sugar and sweeteners. Heather thanked him.

'It's so civilised in here these days,' she said to Max. 'What about you? Are you busy?'

'A lot of routine surveillance work. Corporate stuff. Boring as hell. Now, tell me, to what do I owe the pleasure of your company this morning?' He looked at the clock above the bar. 'I mean, this afternoon. Thank God I'm not drinking in the morning. You still not drinking, then?'

Heather nodded, smiling.

'That's great. Now, why did you call me?'

'Do I need a reason to want to see you? OK, I know it's been a while. Actually, something's worrying me, and I wanted to talk to you about it, see what you think.'

'Fire away.'

'I was seeing this young girl in the centre – young woman, I should say, early thirties – and she fell from the balcony of her flat and died. The police are saying she fell or jumped. She'd been drinking. They say no-one else was there.'

'And you feel somehow to blame, that you should have been able to prevent it.'

'I don't know about that...'

'Well, don't, Heather. You can't save everybody. Maybe you can't save anybody. You see damaged people for one hour a week and expect to work miracles.'

'Thank you, I could've got that crap advice from my manager,' said Heather. 'Maybe I feel I could've missed something, could've done better by her, but it's not that. I wonder if it wasn't an accident or suicide. I wonder if someone else was involved.'

'Do you have a suspect?'

'A couple of suspects actually. One in particular is out in front.'

'And the police? What are they doing?'

'They don't think it's a suspicious death, so they've left it with the coroner. I want to get the police back on the case.'

Heather pushed the plunger down in the cafetière, poured coffee into the cup and added milk.

'Who's the officer in charge of the investigation?' asked Max.

'DI John Kelly. Do you know him?'

'Yeah, I do. Good, thorough cop. They're overstretched these days – insufficient manpower to follow up every lead. But he's a decent guy. He wouldn't neglect to investigate a young woman's death if there was anything suspicious, so there probably wasn't. Who's this main suspect of yours?'

'Her ex-boyfriend. I met him at the funeral.'

Max raised his eyebrows.

'Yes, I went to Phoebe's funeral. The boyfriend hadn't accepted that she'd finished with him, and he'd been violent towards her. Remind me what happens now with the coroner.'

'They did a post-mortem, I assume.'

Heather nodded.

'And then released the body for burial.'

'She was cremated,' said Heather.

'Right. The coroner will have opened the inquest and adjourned it to hold an investigation. If suicide is suspected, there's always going to be a hearing. The inquest is supposed to be resumed within six months, but you'll be lucky if it is. You might be called as a witness.'

'I don't want to wait around for six months. I want to persuade John Kelly to look at this again. I'm thinking of talking to the ex-boyfriend, see if I can get him to open up. And I might visit the mother – I only had a brief chat with her at the funeral.'

'You never know, the investigation might unearth something that makes the coroner suspect foul play. You may not need to stick your neck out at all.'

'You think I'll be sticking my neck out if I look into this myself?'

'Of course you will. The police won't appreciate your attempts to do a Miss Marple. Anyway, you're her therapist. It's not your job to look into it.' Max lifted his glass and gulped down the last of the Guinness. 'Boundaries, isn't that what you lot talk about all the time?'

'Phoebe's dead, Max. All I can think about is that she's dead and I need to find out what happened to her.'

'Is this about Phoebe? Or is it about you?'

Heather wanted to protest and stopped herself.

'I need another drink,' said Max. He placed his hands on the table and leant on it to lift himself from his seat.

'I'll get you one,' said Heather. 'Same again?'

Heather stood at the bar waiting for the Guinness.

Phoebe did remind her of her younger self in some ways, but she was annoyed that Max had suggested this was about her. She returned to the table with his drink.

'What makes you ask if it's about me?'

'Have any of your other clients died?'

'Yes, I've had two other clients who died. One died of cancer and the other was a heroin overdose.'

Max took a drink, and Heather poured the last of her coffee into her cup.

'You think I should leave it alone,' said Heather.

'If you think there's something not right here, then maybe there is. I might be tempted to go for it, but you've got other considerations. Like your career, for instance.'

'I don't think I can leave it alone, Max.'

He was silent for a moment, his bright-blue eyes fixed on her. 'I guess you won't rest unless you've done your best for this lass.' He sighed. 'Just be careful.'

Heather breathed out. She hadn't realised she was holding her breath.

'Did you have trouble standing up just now?' she asked.

'It's rheumatoid arthritis. I went to the doctor and got a hospital referral. They've given me some tablets and told me I should stop smoking, or the tablets won't work so well.'

'You'd better stop smoking, then.'

'What do you think this is?' He waved the plastic inhalator at her, brought it to his lips and sucked on it. 'It's fucking rubbish.'

'Are you using it right?'

'It's rubbish, I tell you.'

'Get some proper advice, for God's sake, Max.'

4

Heather was sitting next to Martin in a pub in Shepherd's Bush, her camel coat between them on the bench seat.

'What's that you're drinking?'

'Appletiser,' said Heather.

'Don't you drink alcohol?'

'No. I used to, but I don't now.'

The décor was dark – dark wood; dark, patterned carpet; maroon walls and curtains. A one-armed bandit was a bright splash of moving colours at one end of the bar. It was early evening and a few customers, mainly men and a few women, stood in groups with drinks or sat alone on bar stools.

'Is that for health reasons?'

Martin looked less gaunt than when Heather had last seen him. His hair had been cut, his black T-shirt looked clean, if a bit crumpled.

'You could say that,' said Heather. 'I used to drink too much so I thought I'd better stop.'

Martin appraised her with his green eyes, his expression serious.

'You said you wanted to talk about Phoebe,' he said.

'I thought you might want to talk about her,' said Heather. 'I could see how upset you were at the funeral.'

'You never said, when we met, you know, at the funeral, who you actually are,' said Martin. 'Like why you were there, how you know Phoebe. Thanks for the drink, though.'

He picked up his pint of bitter and drank half of it in one draught.

'I knew her through work,' said Heather.

Martin glared at her. 'She changed when she went to work at that mental health charity. They turned her against me, the people at that place.'

'Oh, I'm sure they didn't,' said Heather. 'They wouldn't do that.'

'They stopped her from taking my calls.'

'Well, maybe that's because we're not encouraged to spend time on personal calls during work hours. It's the same in any workplace.'

'Did Phoebe tell you about me?' said Martin. 'Did she tell you I was too full on? That's what she said to me, that I was too full on. I hope she also told you that I looked after her when she was pissed and depressed, and cooked meals for her and that I was loyal, something I don't think she knew the meaning of, by the way.'

'I know the relationship she had with you was important to her.'

'So important she wanted to have a break from me,' said Martin. He took another large swig of his beer. 'I'm going out for a cigarette.'

The pub was filling up. Martin put on a black coat that

had been on the seat next to him and pushed through the crowd to the door.

Heather took her mobile out of her bag. No new texts, but there was an email from a friend she hadn't seen for a while. She would reply later. She put the phone on the table. Would Martin open up to her now he thought she was Phoebe's colleague? She felt clumsy and inexperienced in this undercover role, uncomfortable with the deception required.

Martin came back with another pint, threw his coat onto the bench seat and sat down, opposite Heather this time.

'She talked to you a lot, did she?' said Martin. 'Was it in the office you had these conversations, or did you spend time together outside as well?'

'We had coffee and lunch together a few times. She was only there a short time, but we hit it off and I liked her a lot. That's why I wanted to attend the funeral – for myself and on behalf of all her other colleagues who couldn't make it.' She realised colleagues might have been there; if so, she hadn't come across any of them.

'She was seeing a therapist,' said Martin. 'She wouldn't tell me what she talked about, she just said she talked about herself.'

'How did you feel about that?' asked Heather.

'You sound like a therapist.'

Heather shrugged. 'Sorry about that. I work with counsellors, it rubs off.'

'You know how it goes, then,' said Martin. 'How did I feel? Did I feel excluded and insecure and that she might be talking about me?'

'Well, you might have felt like that,' said Heather. 'Did you?'

'As a matter of fact I did, yes.'

Martin picked up a beer mat, turned it on its edge and tapped on the table with it in time to the music playing in the background. It was "Whiskey in the Jar" by Thin Lizzy.

'Phoebe told me you're a good musician,' said Heather. 'What do you play?'

'Piano, guitar. Phoebe sang when I played guitar sometimes.'

'Did she have a good voice?'

'Not bad. She could hold a tune, as my dad would say. We were working on setting some of her poems to music. Then she said we should cool it for a while.' Martin sat up straight and fixed his eyes on Heather. 'Did you tell her she should finish with me?'

'Goodness, no. Why would I do that?'

'Well, you're older than Phoebe. Not much, of course.' His smile was disarming. 'But you are older and maybe she looked to you for advice?'

'Hmm, I wouldn't say I'm qualified to give advice about relationships. I'm a good listener, that's all.'

'OK, when you were listening to Phoebe, did she say why she wanted to "cool it" with me? She must've talked about it.'

'I can't help you there,' said Heather. 'Perhaps you have an idea yourself about why it was.'

Martin looked thoughtful for a moment and then took a swig of beer.

'You said you don't get on with Phoebe's friends,' said Heather, 'but you didn't elaborate.'

'Did I say that?'

'Yes, at the funeral.'

'Oh, it's nothing really. They're OK. Phoebe would've come back to me. I think she knew no-one would ever love her like I do.'

'How did she die, Martin? How did it happen?'

'It was my fault. I should've saved her... but she'd been pushing me away.'

Heather could see her mobile out of the corner of her eye; if only she had found out how to record a conversation with a phone. She swore to herself.

'What happened that night?' she said, her voice almost a whisper.

'How the fuck should I know?' said Martin. He saw that a woman at the next table had turned to listen and lowered his voice. 'I wasn't there. How many times do I have to repeat this to the police, to you? I wasn't fucking there.'

'You said it was your fault, just now.'

'I do blame myself,' he said. He let out a sigh and his shoulders dropped. 'Of course I do. She was the love of my life, and I shouldn't have let it happen.'

'The police questioned you, then?'

'They sure did. I helped them with their enquiries. I told them it must've been an accident. But I can't know for sure, because I wasn't there.'

'The coroner will investigate now,' said Heather.

'Is that right?'

'Would you like another pint?' said Heather. 'I won't have another – I can only drink one of these fizzy things and I'll need to be off anyway in a minute.'

'Yeah, thanks.'

Heather had to wait to be served. She made sure she got in when it was her turn – she was well-practised at that. She felt she wouldn't get any further with Martin now but wanted to part on good terms so he would agree to meet her again. She wanted to mull over their conversation when she was alone.

Martin had moved back to the bench seat where he'd been sitting when she arrived. Heather placed the glass of beer in front of him and thanked him for meeting with her. She put on her coat, and as she said goodbye, she placed a hand on his arm, just for a second.

Am I a hypocrite now? she asked herself as she left the pub. *Have I become manipulative and ruthless?* Strangely, she felt this was not entirely the case, because she had some sympathy for Martin. He was vulnerable, and had she not been focused on her quest to find out what happened to Phoebe, she felt she could care about what happened to him.

5

On Saturday morning, Heather hired a car and drove out of London into Surrey. She arrived in Farnham at lunchtime, had a sandwich in a café and drew up outside Phoebe's mother's house in the early afternoon. She rang the front doorbell and saw, through the frosted glass, a woman coming through the hall.

'Hello, Jean. Do you remember me? I'm Heather. I came to Phoebe's funeral.'

Jean was wearing a flower-print top and black trousers. It appeared to take her a moment to recognise Heather.

'Of course. Sorry, I wasn't sure where I'd met you.'

'I was taking a drive and ended up near you, so I thought I'd call in, on the off-chance you'd be at home. I hope you don't mind.'

'Well, I'm usually out shopping by this time but I'm running late.'

'I don't want to hold you up.'

'No, please, come in.'

Heather stepped inside and followed Jean into the lounge. Jean offered tea and went into the kitchen to make

37

it. Heather sat on a dark-blue sofa, part of a three-piece suite arranged around a tiled coffee table. She looked around the room. Behind her, towards the window, on an upright piano, stood a framed photograph of Phoebe, the one that was on the front of the order of the service booklet – Phoebe as a young woman with shoulder-length, honey-blonde hair. On a sideboard opposite the sofa were two more framed prints – a baby photo and the one of Phoebe as a schoolgirl in uniform. Heather went over and picked up the schoolgirl photo. She had this photo in her hand when Jean came from the kitchen with mugs of tea.

'How old would Phoebe be here?' asked Heather.

Jean put the mugs on the coffee table and took the photo from Heather.

'She'd be eleven or twelve. It was before my husband Tom died, Phoebe's father. She was very much a daddy's girl.'

Jean replaced the photo on the sideboard, handed Heather a mug of tea and sat in one of the armchairs.

'Tom died of lung cancer,' she said. 'He was a journalist, up against deadlines all the time. He drank like a fish and smoked like a chimney.'

Heather nodded and took a sip of tea. 'What work do you do, Jean?'

'I work in a health centre, administration. You worked with Phoebe, didn't you say?'

'Yes, she was doing well, supporting clients to live independently.'

'People with mental health problems?'

'Yes.'

'She'd have a feel for that,' said Jean.

'She did, yes,' said Heather.

'I can't get it out of my mind, you know,' said Jean, 'that she might have killed herself. She must have been very unhappy, and she didn't feel she could come home. My mother is devastated; she's become frail overnight, confused. How Phoebe could do that to us I'll never know. I'm sorry, I haven't really had anyone to talk to about this.'

'I find it difficult to believe she killed herself,' said Heather. 'I'm puzzled by her death, as well as sad.'

Jean nodded several times, her eyes on Heather.

'Do you think it was an accident, then?'

'It might have been,' said Heather. 'She didn't seem depressed to me. I'm hoping the inquest will shed light on what happened.'

Jean shivered. 'I'm dreading the inquest,' she said. 'But of course I shall go.'

They were both silent for a few minutes.

'Did Phoebe have a boyfriend?' asked Jean.

'There was someone,' said Heather, 'Martin, the young man who came late to the funeral.'

Jean frowned, trying to remember.

'But she'd finished with him,' said Heather, 'as far as I know. Phoebe talked about her father and also a stepfather. Is his name Alan?'

Jean smiled. 'Hmm, Alan. My second husband. Looking back, I suppose I married again too soon. It was just two years after Tom died.'

'You feel it was too soon? For you, you mean?'

'And for Phoebe. I think Phoebe felt shut out. I wasn't there for her.'

'You were grieving,' said Heather.

'I was. And in the end I drove Alan away because he could never be Tom.'

'Do you keep in touch with Alan?'

'Not really. I did tell him Phoebe had died. He was going to come to the funeral and then there was some sort of emergency. I see him around town. And I'm always seeing his van – it seems to be there wherever I go. I got one of his leaflets through the door the other day – there it is, under the table.'

Heather reached down to the shelf under the coffee table and picked up a flyer. It advertised loft conversions, kitchen extensions, patios, built at competitive prices by Alan Ramsey and Sons. There was a phone number and a website.

'I'll put it in the recycling,' said Jean. She held out her hand. Heather handed Jean the leaflet and she put it on the arm of her chair.

'It's good to talk to someone who knew Phoebe,' said Jean. 'I can't talk to my friends about her. They seem embarrassed. They just want to cheer me up, always inviting me to, I don't know, exercise classes, coffee mornings, dinner, and I don't want to go.'

'Losing a child is too painful for them to contemplate, I suppose,' said Heather.

'It's not just that,' said Jean. 'I wasn't close to Phoebe, and I think they find me cold.'

'You could ask your doctor about bereavement counselling.'

'Would that help, do you think?'

'It might.'

'Would you like some more tea? I didn't offer you a biscuit.'

Heather spread her hands and shook her head.

'I'll see if I have any,' said Jean.

As she stood up, Alan's leaflet slipped off the arm of the chair and floated to the floor. Jean went into the kitchen. Heather took her phone from her bag, went over and picked up the leaflet and took a photo of it. She replaced it on the arm of the chair as Jean returned with some chocolate digestives on a plate. Heather sat on the sofa again, looked at her phone as if checking for messages and put it back in her bag.

'Thank you,' said Heather. 'The tea was very welcome, but I've cut out biscuits. I'm trying to lose weight. I'll be making a move soon. Are you going into town to do your shopping? Can I give you a lift?'

'I'm not quite ready,' said Jean.

'I can wait for you. May I use your loo before I go, please?'

In Jean's bathroom, Heather recalled the last time she'd been there, the day of the funeral, how she'd wanted to linger in that turquoise and white space and avoid going downstairs, but people were waiting to come in. Today, Jean had opened up to her just as Martin had, to some extent, and of course it was because they both wanted to talk about Phoebe. Was she taking advantage of them and their grief? Yes, she was, but she hoped she could justify it in terms of her search for the truth about Phoebe's death.

Heather dropped Jean off in the main shopping area of the town and went in search of somewhere to park. She wanted to look on her phone at the photo of Alan's flyer and find his business address.

When she got home, Heather changed her bedclothes. She'd meant to do it in the morning and hadn't had time. And she wanted something physical to do after sitting in the car. It was satisfying to shake out the fresh-smelling fitted sheet, pull it tight over the corners and tuck it in, to push the double duvet into the clean cover and billow it out, once, twice, three times until the corners and sides of the cover were evenly filled. Finally, she put on the clean pillowcases. The bed, immaculate in its pink, orange and purple floral cover, was inviting. Clean sheets, fresh start? She straightened the items on her bedside cabinet – lamp, books, notebook, pen, hand cream, coaster – looking for a sense of order, to calm her and renew her resolve.

She hadn't been able to contact Phoebe's stepfather, Alan. There was no business address on the website and when she'd called the mobile number, she'd reached his voicemail. What message could she leave? She'd been overwhelmed with a feeling of impotence and a sense of the futility of her quest. If she had contacted Alan, what could she have said to him? How could she explain her presence in Farnham and her reasons for wanting to talk to him? 'I used to work with Phoebe, and I'm not satisfied with the police explanation for what happened to her so I'm looking into it myself and I thought you might be able to help.' It sounded ridiculous.

After dinner – a baked potato with tuna and sweetcorn and salad – she watched an episode of *Inspector Montalbano* on television. It was a convoluted tale with multiple red herrings and the distractions of long-distance romance, delicious meals, a sprinkling of farce and the beautiful buildings and bay of Vigata. *People take holidays*, she reminded herself. She could book a trip to Sicily in the spring. As for romance, she wondered later, as she got into bed, whether there would ever again be someone in the bed with her. It was two years since she'd broken up with Daniel, her most recent partner, or rather, they had drifted apart after he'd accepted a new academic post in Liverpool. They'd seen each other less and less until they didn't see each other at all. Unlike Salvo Montalbano and his Livia, they hadn't managed to sustain their long-distance relationship.

6

Heather woke on Sunday morning in her clean sheets and found herself thinking about her own stepfather, Phillip. She didn't want to think about him; she had a vague feeling he had featured in her dream, as a minor character, but there all the same. Heather's stepfather experience had not been good. She couldn't understand what her mother saw in Phillip; he seemed colourless and boring compared with her father, James Delaney, who was dark and good-looking, with a lot of charm and also a lot of demons and an alcohol problem. Phillip hadn't touched her inappropriately, but he had made slightly lecherous remarks that made her feel uncomfortable. She was sixteen when he'd appeared on the scene, and he had said she was growing up into a lovely young woman "with curves in all the right places". He said his secretary had long legs, but Heather's legs were "more shapely", and she should show them off. It disgusted her to think that he was looking at her that way. He'd invited her out to lunch a couple of times and she'd made excuses.

Her mother, Sonia, had seemed oblivious to Phillip's

roving eye. She worked long hours; she had her man to come home to and go to garden centres and DIY stores with at the weekend and to attend dinner parties and entertain with. She exhorted Heather to do well at school so she would "have more choices" and was scathing if presented with a less than perfect school report. Heather had always done her best to oblige with excellent reports and good exam grades. Sonia was a bit more easy-going with Heather's younger brother, Anthony.

Heather got up and dressed, sorted her laundry and put on a wash. She enjoyed breakfast every day and especially at the weekend, when she could take her time. She made poached eggs, toast and tea, and ate at the dining table with the Saturday *Guardian* propped against a pile of folders.

As she cleared the table and washed the dishes, her thoughts turned again to Phoebe's stepfather Alan. He appeared to have done the honourable thing when Phoebe had flung herself at him when she was drunk at her mother's house. He had come to see her in London after that. What had happened during that visit?

She watered her indoor plants – an ancient rubber plant, a cheese plant, peace lilies. By then the wash was done, so she hung her damp clothes on airers and coat hangers, shaking out the creases. And then she took out her notes, her sessions with Phoebe.

Alan had visited Phoebe during the time when she was still seeing Martin. Heather found the session. She'd told Heather it had felt strange and uncomfortable, Alan being there in her space.

'*He seemed big,*' Phoebe had said, '*larger than life.*'

Heather had asked if she felt threatened and she'd said no, but he was very manly.

'No-one could get me whilst he was there,' she'd said.

Heather had noted that the expression *get me* was like something from a game or a horror movie.

Alan had taken Phoebe for lunch at an Italian restaurant, and they'd had pasta and wine. He'd asked if she was seeing anyone and she'd told him about Martin and that he was a musician, but she didn't tell him that Martin was becoming jealous and possessive. Alan had urged her to contact her mother, said her mother was missing her. He had also confided that that he didn't know whether he could make her mother happy. Phoebe told Heather that she thought he was right, and her mother was missing Phoebe's father, who had been the love of her life. But she hadn't said this to Alan.

How did it end? According to her notes, they'd parted outside the restaurant and Alan had said, *'Look after yourself.'* Nothing worrying there, but the notes were unusually brief and sketchy, short on interpretation. Why was that? Had Phoebe come late to the session? Was Heather rushing off somewhere afterwards? She had a twinge of guilt, wondering if she'd missed something.

Perhaps Alan had come to London again, looking for a sympathetic ear, if his relationship with Jean was in trouble. Perhaps Phoebe had not been so discrete and sensitive the next time. Perhaps, on that next occasion, if she was upset about Martin's behaviour and had been drinking, she had looked to Alan for physical comfort.

Heather looked at Alan's website again and sent an email enquiry saying she wanted an extension built and asking if he took on work in West London. She said he'd been recommended by a friend. He replied quickly that yes, he took jobs in London and would be in her area on Thursday. Heather had no clients to see on Thursday morning, so she arranged a time for Alan to visit.

She switched off her laptop. She was making progress; Alan was actually coming to her. She had time to decide what to say about Phoebe. Regarding the extension, she had thought about having one and would say she wanted to know what was viable but wouldn't want to start work on it until the spring.

In the afternoon, she went to Tate Britain with a friend. It was only in the evening, when she was alone at home and the Sunday evening blues were setting in, that she started to have cold feet. If she suspected Alan in the least, why had she invited him to her home?

As Thursday approached, Heather was nervous. She wanted to say as little as possible about her relationship with Phoebe; she continued to feel uncomfortable about what she was doing and the subterfuge involved.

She spent some time sketching a plan of what she'd had in mind when she was interested in having an extension built on the back of her house. It would extend the kitchen and give her a sunny lounging or eating area, with folding glass doors opening on to a patio. Why on earth had she thought about this? She must have been bored.

On Thursday morning, she saw Alan's white van pull up outside, right on time at eleven o'clock. It was the van Jean had mentioned seeing around Farnham, with Alan Ramsey and Sons on the side. She opened the front door. Alan came up the path with a clipboard and a briefcase. He was fiftyish, about five foot eleven with a muscular build and a pleasant, sun-tanned face, thinning brown hair and blue eyes. He was wearing a navy-blue showerproof bomber jacket and grey trousers. He put down the briefcase and held out his hand.

'Ms Delaney? Alan Ramsey. Pleased to meet you.'

As they walked through the hall to the kitchen, Heather began to understand what Phoebe had meant about him being large and having a very masculine presence. She offered him tea or coffee and he asked for coffee with sugar, so she reached for her large cafetière.

'I really just want your opinion about what's possible,' she said. 'I've done a drawing. I can get it.'

'Yes, show me what you've got in mind,' he said. 'May I have a look outside?'

She showed him out of the back door and could see him through the window, surveying the back of the house. She let the water cool a little before pouring it into the cafetière, and then fetched her drawing. She went outside, placed the two mugs of coffee on the metal table outside the French window, handed her drawing to Alan and explained her thoughts about the project.

'Not a bad drawing,' he said, with a smile. 'That's all perfectly feasible, I think.'

Heather noted that his manner was relaxed, and whilst he gave the impression of being an old-fashioned man, a "man's man", he didn't talk down to her.

He showed her photographs of extensions he'd built before, and then took a metal tape from his briefcase and measured the existing crazy paved patio and how far the kitchen extended out. He asked to be shown into the house and examined the back walls and windows from the inside. They both came back outside, and he asked if he could take photographs. Heather said yes and he spent some time getting shots of the back of the house from different angles.

'You don't want to extend the first floor as well?' he asked.

'Hmm, I hadn't thought about doing that.'

He strode onto the lawn and looked back at the house and up at the roof.

'You could build upwards, you know, if you wanted to,' he said.

Heather joined Alan on the lawn and looked up at her roof.

'A lot of householders in properties like this are making a room in the roof space and it can come out over the ground and first-floor extension.'

'I don't know,' said Heather. 'I don't have children. I'm not sure I would need that.'

His eyes met hers and he smiled. There were deep laughter lines at the corners of his eyes and his smile was reassuring, kind.

'It's an option, and it would enhance the value of your property. Of course, you'd need planning permission before any of these works could go ahead.'

'Yes, I know, thank you,' said Heather. 'Mr Ramsey, I have to tell you something.' She paused, nervous about what his reaction would be. 'I knew your stepdaughter, Phoebe,' she said.

He moved his head backwards slightly but held her

gaze. What was it that she could see in his eyes now? Shock? Sadness? Fear?

'You knew Phoebe?'

'I worked with her, yes. She recommended you.'

'What?' The relaxed, friendly manner was gone.

'I mentioned to her that I was thinking about having an extension built and she said why not contact you. But that's not the point now.'

'The poor kid killed herself,' said Alan, 'you know that, don't you?'

'Yes, I'm sorry. I can see I've upset you.'

Alan walked back towards the house and Heather followed him. He picked up his tape and put it in his briefcase.

'There are local builders who can do this job for you,' he said. 'If you actually want an extension built, that is.'

'I do, yes. But I want to talk about Phoebe as well and perhaps you do too.'

'Why the hell would I want to talk to you about her? I don't know you from Adam.'

The mugs of coffee were untouched on the table. Heather picked one up and held it out to Alan.

'Two sugars,' she said. 'Look, I got quite close to Phoebe, and I was totally shocked when she died. I went to the funeral. I didn't see you there.'

Alan hesitated and then took the coffee. 'I didn't make it. I should have, for Jean, Phoebe's mother.' He took a sip of coffee as if on autopilot.

'Were you close to Phoebe?' asked Heather.

He shot her a warning look. 'She was Jean's daughter,' he said. 'She was a bit mixed-up. I felt protective towards her, but close? No.'

'I'm sorry if it seems like I got you here under false pretences,' said Heather, 'but I'm trying to talk to people who knew Phoebe because I don't believe she killed herself or that it was an accident.'

'Can't you just let the police do their job?' said Alan.

'They're not doing their job. They've passed the case to the coroner because they don't think it's a criminal matter. Please, Mr Ramsey, Alan. You visited Phoebe in London a few months ago and bought her lunch. An Italian restaurant, she said.'

Alan put down the coffee and picked up his briefcase and clipboard.

'You two obviously had a better relationship than I had with my stepfather,' said Heather.

'Really?' said Alan. 'I assume I can get out down the side of the house, can I?'

'There's something I have to ask,' she said. 'Please, can you just tell me, did you see Phoebe more recently in London?'

Alan moved to leave, and Heather stepped forward, almost blocking his way.

'The reason I ask,' she continued, 'is because I was deeply shocked by her death, and I wondered if you knew her state of mind. I know she had split up with her boyfriend, Martin, and he found it difficult to accept.'

She stepped back and Alan walked past the kitchen window towards the side of the house.

'Martin was stalking her, Alan.'

He turned and glared at her.

'He's a toerag,' he said. 'I think you should get some help, Ms Delaney, counselling or something.'

51

'Did you meet him? Did you meet Martin?'

Heather watched Alan walk down the side of the house and a few moments later she heard him drive away. Her legs were shaking. She sat on a metal chair next to her cold coffee.

7

'Rosemary doesn't apologise as much as she did when she started,' said Heather to her supervisor, Val. 'That's a result, I think.'

'Indeed!' said Val.

They were sitting in armchairs in a small consulting room on the second floor of the centre. Like Heather's room, it overlooked the gardens in the square. They each had a mug of peppermint tea on the low table between them. Val's slightly frizzy brown hair was cut in a bob, and she wore a navy smock top and loose linen trousers.

'She's booked a holiday with one of those single traveller companies,' said Heather. 'She made the decision to do it, and she's doing something for herself. Also, she said no to babysitting when she had something arranged, which was a major thing for her; she was very anxious about it and relieved when she found her son and daughter-in-law were still speaking to her. So she's doing well, gaining confidence.'

'That's good,' said Val. She put on her glasses and looked at the notes on her lap. 'What's happening with David?'

'David is very stressed at work because a member of staff left and was not replaced, so his workload has increased. His wife works for the same company, and this doesn't help, even though she's in a different department. He's finding it difficult to control his eating and he's still evacuating his pain, rather than facing it. And he's spending more time at his mother's, which he knows is not a good idea. We're working through what he might do to alleviate the work situation and reduce his dependence on his mother.'

'What's David's wife like? Is she supportive?' asked Val.

'I think she wants to be supportive. According to David, she's very confident and efficient and she manages staff, so perhaps she tries to manage him. He feels he can't match up to her, and this adds to his discomfort at work. It would help if one of them got a new job.'

Val smiled.

'David is looking,' said Heather. 'I'd like to tell you about a new client.'

'Yes, please do.'

'I assessed a woman last week, Naomi, and I felt quite uncomfortable with her. She was very tense and controlled and spoke very loudly. And she stared at me throughout.'

'What's her psychiatric history?'

'She's fifty-eight and has had a diagnosis of bipolar disorder and also of psychotic depression and she's on anti-psychotic medication. She's been hospitalised several times.'

'Who referred her for psychotherapy?'

'Her psychiatrist,' said Heather. 'She has a husband

who is a lot older than her, quite elderly. She's his carer now because he's got a lot of health problems.'

'Do you feel she could benefit from therapy at present?'

'I'm not sure. But I want to see if I can help her. The husband has been physically violent and probably emotionally abusive as well. She needs support. At the end of the session, as I was showing her out, she grabbed my wrist, which gave me a bit of a fright – she looked so desperate and wild-eyed.'

'She may need support, but it doesn't necessarily have to be you who provides it for her,' said Val. 'And psychotherapy may not be her best option. What do you want to do?'

'I want to see her again, maybe have an extended assessment period.'

'That sounds reasonable. Let's make sure we talk about her again next time. If you'd like to bring your notes from a session,' said Val, 'it'll give us a concrete starting point when we're talking about her.'

'Yes. I'll do that.'

Val took a drink of her tea. Heather reached out, picked up her own tea and took a sip. It was lukewarm but refreshing.

'What about the young woman who died. Phoebe?' said Val. 'Last time we met, you were not ready to talk much about what happened. I know it affected you deeply. You did say you were finding it difficult to accept the view of the police that it was an accident or suicide.'

'I still feel the same. I think it's unlikely that it was an accident and as I said before, her mood was improved. She hadn't expressed suicidal thoughts, let alone intentions.'

'Could it have been an impulsive act?' asked Val. She put down her mug.

'At that time, things were going well for her, so I don't think so.'

'How do you think you'll feel if the coroner concludes that it was suicide?'

Heather turned towards the window and gazed out at the tops of the trees in the square. The leaves were brown, russet and yellow; they were loosening and falling; winter was coming.

'It would be terrible for her family,' she said.

'How would you feel?'

Heather turned back to face Val. 'Angry, I expect.'

'What would it mean for you if it was, in fact, suicide?'

Heather gave a short laugh. 'I should hand in my notice,' she said, 'because I obviously didn't know Phoebe and I should have done. And I should have picked up on something.'

'You'd been seeing her for how long?' said Val. 'Ten weeks?'

'Yes. It's not long, I know.'

'But you felt you knew her.'

Heather nodded and shifted in her chair.

'It's clear you established a good rapport with Phoebe,' said Val. 'Did you feel more of a connection with her than with other clients?'

'Yes. I've thought about it, and it is partly because she reminded me of myself when I was younger.'

'Could you elaborate?' Val looked over her glasses.

'I told you before that I had an alcohol problem.'

Val nodded.

'I've been sober for eleven years now,' said Heather. 'There's the drinking, and some other similarities, like not being very close to my mother, having had to deal with a stepfather, making unwise choices when it came to boyfriends, partners.'

'You said you had to deal with a stepfather.'

'I just mean coping with some other man coming in where your father should be.'

'Forgive me if you've told me and I've forgotten,' said Val. 'Did your father die?'

'My parents separated. I saw my father sometimes. I still see him. He lives in Nottingham.'

'OK, there's quite a lot of shared experience with Phoebe and this can be helpful in terms of giving you some insight into what is going on with your client, but it can also make it difficult to disentangle yourself from her, from this case. Perhaps there was some split off part of Phoebe that you didn't know about. I read a very useful paper on splitting recently, I can forward it to you.' Val leant forward, her head slightly to one side. 'Shall I do that?'

'I don't suppose you'll approve,' said Heather, 'but I went to Phoebe's funeral.'

'OK. Did that help in coming to terms with what happened?'

'Not really, no.'

'What do you think happened to Phoebe?'

'I think someone else was involved and the police should be investigating.'

'Do you want to tell me who you think was involved?'

'No,' said Heather. 'I can't be sure.' She usually

appreciated Val's feedback and support but had no wish to talk to her anymore about Phoebe.

Val placed her file of notes on the table and her hands on the arms of her chair.

'I understand that you feel angry,' she said. 'At the inquest, the coroner will reach a conclusion, and I hope you'll be able to accept it and move on. In the meantime, I would suggest you take your feelings about Phoebe to your own therapist, to help you reflect on them and manage them, because I think you're struggling to make sense of those feelings.'

'I'm not in therapy at the moment,' said Heather.

'You might like to consider it,' said Val. 'It might be helpful for you.'

There was a ticking, tapping sound coming from the window and a swishing from the road below. Heather looked out again. It was raining, and each pane of the sash window was covered in droplets, some still and clinging to the glass and some coursing down like tears.

'Heather?'

Heather turned back to Val.

'I'll send you that paper,' said Val. 'Is there anyone else you want to talk about today?'

8

Heather was unnerved by her confrontation with Alan Ramsey. It hadn't been too difficult meeting with Jean and Martin as they had wanted to talk to her about Phoebe. Martin had been defensive but not hostile. Alan had been hostile. What happened with him had made her realise she needed a thicker skin if she was going to pursue this investigation. When she was younger she'd desperately wanted people to like her, a bit like her client Rosemary, always wanting to please people and finding it difficult to say no. Drinking had enabled her to care a bit less about what people thought, but the hangover brought paranoia and shame, feelings worse than those she had sought to escape. Since she'd stopped drinking, she had grown in confidence and developed more resilience, but sometimes she still felt that need to be liked creeping in. She knew she could do with some support and guidance, so she called Max. He invited her to his place for dinner on Friday.

On Friday evening, Heather rang Max's buzzer, and he let her into the hallway. She climbed the stairs to his first-floor flat and he was waiting at the top, holding the door open for her. She was happy to see his mellow face again. He seemed to be stooping a bit, looked shorter and older somehow. She kissed him on both cheeks; his skin, above the grey stubble, was soft and papery, and there were rosy patches on his cheekbones, as if he had blusher on, or had a fever.

'Max,' she said. 'It's good to see you. Are you OK?'

'I'm fine,' said Max. 'A bit of pain in my joints, but otherwise I'm just dandy. What can I get you to drink? How about some Irn-Bru?'

'Oh, God, full of sugar, but never mind, go on then.'

Max went into the kitchen. He'd laid the dining table with forks and spoons, and put out parmesan, so Heather guessed he was cooking spaghetti. She walked to the far end of the living room; its length was the width of the house, and its two large sash windows were hung with green brocade curtains that had seen better days. There were piles of newspapers on the settee and one of the armchairs; the surfaces were dusty, and the carpet could have done with hoovering. He had a couple of spider plants on the windowsills that were in need of water. On the wooden coffee table in front of the settee was an ashtray with an extinguished roll-up balancing on the side. Next to it was a pack of tobacco, papers, disposable lighter and a small bag of grass.

Max returned with a glass of Irn-Bru for Heather and a lager for himself. He picked up the roll-up from the ashtray and lit it.

'What happened to the white plastic nicotine thing?' asked Heather.

'Fuck that,' said Max.

Heather could tell from the smell of the smoke that the tobacco was enhanced with weed.

'The weed helps with the pain,' he said. He limped over to the window and opened the top a few inches. 'Dinner won't be long.'

Heather moved some newspapers and sat down on the settee. 'Tell me, Max,' she said, 'how do you develop a thick skin?'

'Now, why would you want to do that?' With some puffing and panting, he pulled an armchair nearer to the coffee table. He sat down, placing the ashtray on the arm of the chair. 'You need to be sensitive and empathetic in your line of work, do you not?'

Heather told him about her encounter with Alan Ramsey.

'So I alienated him,' she said, 'and I didn't find out whether he'd ever met Martin, or if he saw Phoebe again before she died. I didn't find out anything. Hopeless. And I was scared, I was shaking like a leaf when he left.'

'The guy was expecting to give you an estimate and get some work out of it,' said Max. 'No wonder he was irritated.'

'He was more than irritated. He was positively hostile.'

'Well,' said Max, 'you did learn something.'

'Really?'

'You'll have heard the expression hostile witness. It means a witness in court who is hostile to the party calling them and unwilling to tell the truth, so the questioning brief may have to ask leading questions.'

'Ah, like what? Did you push Phoebe off the balcony of her flat on the night of whatever?'

'Not exactly but leading that way. Where were you on the night in question? How would you describe your relationship with the deceased?'

'I did ask if he was close to Phoebe,' said Heather.

'That would've put his back up, right enough. And it's a closed question. You want to ask open questions.'

'Of course, yes. What did I learn, then?'

'You learnt something about Alan, like he's touchy about the subject of Phoebe, for whatever reason. Something to hide, possibly. He won't tell the truth readily, but it may be because he's used to keeping his own counsel. He was hostile to you because you tricked him and put him on the spot. And he knows Martin, or at least knows of him.'

'Yes, right,' said Heather. 'I'm not likely to get another crack at him now, though.'

'I don't know. If he's a key player, you might want to try again. As long as you're careful. Let me know if you want me to tag along.'

Max's phone rang. He picked it up off the table and went to the kitchen to take the call.

Heather leant back and closed her eyes. Dear Max. She felt safe here with him. He made her feel that the problems she was coming up against were challenges, puzzles that could be solved with the right know-how and a more relaxed, open attitude. He had even offered to come with her to meet Alan. Max's voice through the wall was lilting, familiar.

After about five minutes, he finished the call and put his head round the door.

'Sorry about that. Possible client. I'm sorting the dinner now.'

'Can I have some water, please?' she asked. 'Your plants are wilting.'

She went to the kitchen door, and he handed her a pint glass of water. She poured some of it into the plant pots.

A few more minutes and he carried in two plates of spaghetti Bolognese. Heather joined Max at the dining table and sat opposite him. She realised she was hungry. She added black pepper and parmesan and began to twirl spaghetti on to her fork.

'Thanks, Max. I've missed your spag bol.'

When she'd eaten most of her meal, Heather put down her fork. She leant her elbows on the table and rested her chin on her hands.

'I felt so scared when Alan turned on me,' she said. 'That's why I've been thinking I need a thicker skin.'

'Being scared is par for the course,' said Max. 'You just have to pretend to have a thick skin. Don't your clients ever get angry with you?'

'Of course they do, but it's part of the process, contained in the room. I have the tools to manage it and support to call on if necessary.'

'Exactly,' said Max. 'It's different outside the therapy room, but you still have those tools. You don't need a thicker skin to succeed in this game. What you do need is persistence. Keep at it, whatever people think of you, whatever is thrown at you, don't give up till you find out what you want to know.'

Heather smiled and picked up her fork. Max pushed his plate to one side, the food half eaten, and took a slug of lager.

'What have you got so far?' he asked.

'I went to see Martin, the ex-boyfriend,' said Heather. 'We met in a pub, and he did loosen up a bit. At one point I thought he was telling me he caused her death, but he pulled back.'

Max was about to light a roll-up and paused, lighter in hand. 'What did he say?'

'He said, "It was my fault." Those words. Then he said he should've saved her, but she was pushing him away.'

'Hold on to that,' said Max.

'I wish I'd been able to record the conversation on my phone,' said Heather, 'but I don't know how.'

'I can show you,' said Max. 'I'm visualising them both on the balcony. She's gone out there to get away from him, but he won't leave her alone. She doesn't want him to touch her and she's pushing him away, but he keeps coming and she loses her balance and falls. Or she's threatening to jump, he grabs hold of her and she pushes him away and this makes her lose her balance and fall.'

'Yes, possibly one of those scenarios.'

'You need to imagine all possibilities.'

'But the next minute, Martin was insisting he wasn't there,' said Heather. 'He said he blamed himself because he should've been able to save her.'

'He would say that. He'd let something slip and had to cover his tracks.'

'I should go and see him again, then.'

'Maybe. But could you end up getting into deep water with that one?'

'Why do you say that?'

'I don't know. I have a bad feeling about that young man. Or about you getting involved with him.'

'I don't plan on getting involved with him.'

Max got up, slowly, from the table, limped to the nearest window and drew the curtains.

'Coffee?' he asked.

'Coffee would be great,' said Heather.

She went and drew the curtains across the other window and sat on the settee. Max took the plates into the kitchen and Heather heard him switch the kettle on.

When he returned with the coffees, Heather said, 'I want to talk to DI John Kelly. Do you think he'll see me?'

'He drinks in The White Horse. If you can't get him at the station, you might get him there.'

'Cheers, Max.'

'I got these in for you,' he said. 'They're dark chocolate.' He pushed a box of chocolates across the table.

'You don't half spoil me,' she said.

They chatted about mutual acquaintances at the private investigations agency where Max still worked and compared notes on the state of the world – politics, climate change, crime. He showed her how to record a conversation on her phone. He drank a couple of whiskies and smoked more weed. Heather had another glass of Irn-Bru.

Eventually, she looked at her watch and it was ten thirty.

'Gone are the days when I could crash on this settee,' she said. 'I was grateful for it then, but now I want to go home to my bed. I'll wash the dishes, then I'll be off.'

Max told her to leave the dishes. He called her a taxi and asked the firm to put it on his account.

When the taxi arrived, he insisted on coming downstairs to see Heather off, despite her protestations that there was no need.

At home, she flicked through and rejected the television programmes on offer. She got ready for bed and had a warm feeling of satisfaction from spending a pleasant evening with a trusted friend. It had been useful, too, and had renewed her resolve to continue with the investigation. But there was a nagging fear in the back of her mind that Max was not as well as he made out. She would have to keep an eye on him.

9

Work felt like a distraction, something to keep her busy and get her through time. Every so often, she pulled herself up and reminded herself that she owed each client her full attention. And each was getting it – for fifty minutes – and then she would slip back into Phoebe world. It scared her. She knew she couldn't go on like this indefinitely, or her client work would suffer. Clients would sense any anxiety or lack of attentiveness on her part. And if just one client made a complaint, she would be under scrutiny; it could even lead to her losing her job at the centre and her professional reputation. She needed to get on with finding out what happened to Phoebe; that was the only way to put her own mind at rest and enable her to get on with her life.

As the week went on, Heather thought about what her next move should be. It was too soon to contact Martin again. Could she find Phoebe's friend Sarah and talk to her at more length? If she checked her notes, she might be able to find the name of one of the poetry venues they went to. In the end, she decided to look for DI Kelly and ask him why the police had stopped investigating and handed the case to the coroner. He might not want to talk to her, but she could try. She could at least check out the pub Max had suggested. She would go on Friday, early evening.

She looked up the location of The White Horse online and it was easy to find as it was round the corner from the police station. She arrived outside the pub just after seven o'clock. It was getting dark, and a full moon was rising, large and bright, unnerving, as if a planet were approaching the earth. Elongated clouds scooted across the moon and away across the navy blue sky.

Inside, the pub was dark, with pools of orange lamplight. It was already busy. The bar was on the left and curved round to the left. On the right and straight ahead were wide booths with tables and padded seating, and bar staff were delivering meals to the tables– pie and chips, lasagne, burgers speared with sticks. There was no music, just a clamour of conversation, broken frequently by peals and hoots of laughter. Heather walked around the bar to see if she could spot DI John Kelly.

Beyond the bar there was a small stage in the corner with microphones set up, and a drum kit and keyboard. Heather saw a group of men at the bar who looked like policemen; she couldn't say why, but they did. And then a blonde woman came out of the ladies' toilet and Heather recognised her as the DS who had come with DI John Kelly to interview her, Yvonne Simmonds. Now her hair was loose and shoulder-length, and she was wearing jeans and a black T-shirt. She joined the group of men and picked up a glass of wine from the bar. *Lucky girl*, thought Heather. A glass of wine and all that male company. But maybe they were all male chauvinists and she had to put up with misogynistic banter, or worse.

Heather had no desire to be recognised by Yvonne Simmonds. She pushed open the door to the ladies and surveyed herself in a mirror. Her hair was windswept, so she tidied it with her fingers. Her cheeks were pink, when she wanted to look pale and interesting, so she applied powder, to little effect. She used the toilet, washed her hands and returned to the pub lounge. She went back to the area near the entrance and bought a drink – ginger ale and ice – and looked around for a vantage point. There was room for one person on the end of a seat at the back of the room. She asked the young people at the table if she could sit there, and they smiled and nodded. They were probably colleagues on a Friday night out, the women sharing a bottle of wine and the men on pints.

She sat down, took her phone from her handbag and placed the bag between her feet. From there, she could see the door but didn't think she'd be easily recognisable to anyone coming in. This mattered because she wanted to pick her moment. And she'd decided it would be best to appear to be there for some other reason, rather than on the off-chance that John Kelly would come in. Maybe she could adopt the people on the table as her friends. Or she could be meeting someone who was late. She was tempted to text a friend and ask them to come and meet her. She sipped her drink and scrolled down her contacts. She would decide, when she'd finished this drink, whether to wait longer or leave this as a reconnaissance exercise. She looked at the news on her phone, and then at the weather for the weekend.

She swallowed the last few drops of her drink. Yes, some of his colleagues were here, but that didn't mean John Kelly would be coming; he might not be on duty today. She would leave it for now and go home. She reached for her bag. And then, just as she began to rise from her seat, he came through the door. Heather was surprised to feel her stomach lurch at the sight of him. He was wearing jeans and a brown leather jacket and was unshaven again, brooding, tired-looking. He went straight to the bar, and Heather could just see his back and the right side of his face as he looked for the barman. She would have to act fast if she wanted to catch him before he joined his colleagues. She grabbed her bag, approached him and placed herself next to him at the bar, on his left. She put her hand on his arm, and he turned to see who was there. She remembered his brown eyes from before, the intent look in them, penetrating, alert.

'Well, Ms Delaney. Hello,' he said.

'Heather, please,' she said. She had to raise her voice to be heard. 'I thought it was you. I've been hoping to see you.'

He leant towards her. 'Let me guess,' he said. 'Your client's death. You think you know what happened.'

'Not exactly,' she said. 'I'm sorry to grab you when you're off duty, DI Kelly, but I wasn't sure what to do.'

'It's John. Can I buy you a drink?'

'Ginger ale with ice, thanks.'

He hailed the barman and ordered a pint of bitter and Heather's drink. He was served ahead of other customers who were waiting.

'What can I do for you?' he asked.

He leant towards her again to hear her reply. The difficulty being heard meant she had to be succinct.

'I think someone else was involved.'

'No evidence for it,' he said.

'Her ex-boyfriend, Martin,' she said. 'I think he was there.'

'Yes, he'd been in the flat, but that night?' He shook his head.

Feedback whined from the speakers, someone came on the microphone and announced the act, and the music started up, a cover of "House of the Rising Sun". Trying to talk now was hopeless.

John said something but she didn't catch it.

'Pardon?' She smiled, thinking how pointless her preparation had been for this situation. He smiled too. It was the first time she'd seen him smile.

She tried to ask him if she could have a quick word outside, away from the noise, but he handed her his card and mouthed, 'Call me.'

He picked up his pint and walked off into the crowd, towards where his colleagues were drinking.

Heather slipped the card into her wallet. She took a few sips of her drink and decided to leave the rest. She left the pub and was relieved to be in the cool and relative quiet of the street. There was a bouncer on the door now and he bade her goodnight. The musicians could be heard giving their rendition of the Percy Sledge number "When a Man Loves a Woman". She walked along the street and hailed a black cab. She climbed in, leant back in the cab seat and breathed out, slowly.

Heather had the idea, from television dramas, that plainclothes policemen ate fry-ups in greasy spoon cafés. Or maybe what happened was that the detective bought a big fry-up for the informant. The Half Moon Café, where John Kelly had suggested they meet, was a bit more homely and upmarket than a greasy spoon. The menu outside listed roast dinners, spaghetti Bolognese and steak and chips as well as all-day breakfast, and also panini, ciabattas and sandwiches. Heather was dressed for work in trousers and top, blazer and sensible shoes, but she'd put on a bit of eye make-up. She pushed open the door and saw that John was already there, sitting at a table by the window, looking through some documents. He had reading glasses on and looked mature and studious; she found it an attractive look. He took off the glasses, stood up and shook hands with her. She noted that he was a couple of inches taller than her, and she liked his handshake, firm without being vice-like. She sat down opposite him. He was drinking a small coffee with very little milk. It was mid-afternoon and Heather had drunk enough coffee so she asked the waitress for a breakfast tea. It arrived quickly, a mug of hot water with a teabag on the saucer and a small jug of milk. She dropped the teabag in the mug.

'You found the place, then,' said John. He folded the documents he'd been reading and put them in the inside pocket of his jacket, along with his glasses case.

'Yes, easily, thanks. Do you eat here sometimes?'

'Yeah, the hot meals are good and the toasted sandwiches, and the coffee is just the way I like it.'

'Hmm, it looks strong,' she said. 'They don't know how to make a cup of tea though, do they?'

'I'm afraid not.'

She stirred her tea, pressed the teabag against the side of the mug.

'Thanks for seeing me,' she said.

He had a biro that he held between his fingers, ready for writing, or maybe he'd recently stopped smoking and wanted something to hold.

'You're obviously upset about your client's death,' he said. 'It must be hard for you to accept. Tell me, I'm curious, what makes you think someone else was involved?'

Heather looked around the café. The other customers were eating, reading newspapers or engaged in conversation; the coffee machines hissed and gurgled; the staff repeated orders and clattered cutlery and crockery; and music played in the background at a low volume, Acker Bilk, "Stranger on the Shore". No-one was likely to overhear.

'Phoebe was not suicidal,' she said. 'I'm sure of that. And I don't understand how she could just fall over the balcony if she was there on her own. It doesn't make sense to me. I shouldn't really be telling you this, because it came out in therapy sessions, but her ex-boyfriend Martin was virtually stalking her. He wouldn't accept that she'd finished with him. He would turn up at her flat, follow her home from work. Could he possibly have been there that night? Or someone else, maybe?'

She fished the teabag out of the mug and added milk to her tea.

'All I can do,' said John, in a low voice, 'is tell you how the forensic evidence stacked up. I shouldn't really be doing this, so I won't tell if you won't. First of all, the scene. There were no signs of a struggle in the flat. There was one used wine glass with Phoebe's fingerprints and DNA on it. An empty wine bottle and a half empty wine bottle in the sitting room both had her fingerprints on them and no-one else's. There were fingerprints from various other parties in the flat, including Martin's, but nothing to place anyone there that night. Martin had been there on many occasions, as he said himself, but he had an alibi for that night – he was in a pub, with an acquaintance who vouched for him. As for other possible witnesses, our house-to-house enquires didn't uncover anyone in the vicinity who had seen or heard anything that could help us.'

'I'm surprised no-one around there saw or heard anything,' said Heather. 'What about her phone? There must've been a lot of texts and calls from Martin on it.'

'There were, yes. It was obvious the guy was obsessed. And I remember there was an exchange of texts that night where he asked if he could come over and Phoebe said not tonight.'

'Not tonight,' said Heather, with a sigh and a downward glance, and then she looked up at John again.

'Also,' he said, 'we look at patterns of injuries and her injuries were consistent with falling from a height when drunk.'

'What were they?'

'Are you sure you want to know?'

'Yes.'

'Injuries to the face, brain, spine, internal injuries; for example, a ruptured spleen. Are you OK?'

Heather nodded.

'And the toxicology report indicated a high level of alcohol in her blood,' said John. 'On balance, the evidence suggests accident rather than suicide. I mean the nature of her injuries, and there was no suicide note – there's usually a note.'

Heather put both her hands around her mug of tea. 'Was there anything else?' she said.

'Yes, there's also the victim's history and state of mind; her vulnerability, depression, the alcohol problem.'

'I don't suppose you had access to her GP records, did you?'

'No, we didn't. But the coroner will have access to relevant medical records. Have I convinced you that there was no third party involved, no crime to investigate?'

'No, I'm sorry, you haven't,' said Heather.

John frowned and was silent for a few moments. He twirled the biro between his fingers like a baton. And then he held up his hand and ordered another filter coffee.

'Is this based on a hunch, a matter of intuition?' he asked.

'Kind of,' said Heather, 'but I hope it's also based on insight. I got to know Phoebe quite well in the time she was coming to see me. What would it take for you to reopen the case?'

'New evidence of some kind,' he said.

'What? Like if Martin were to admit to seeing Phoebe that evening, for instance? I've met him, at Phoebe's funeral. I have his number. I could talk to him.'

'I strongly advise you not to do that,' he said. 'It could be risky for you personally and, I would have thought, professionally. When the coroner reconvenes the inquest, you can attend and hear the evidence in full. Leave it to him, or her.'

'And that's supposed to be within six months of the death?'

'Hopefully, yes.'

The waitress brought John's coffee.

'I do appreciate you agreeing to see me,' said Heather. 'Can I ask, why did you meet me and tell me all this?'

John added sugar and a dash of milk to his coffee and stirred it slowly. 'Maybe I care,' he said.

'About what?'

'About a young woman dying and it's not clear how or why, but I had to move on to the next case. And you. You took the trouble to find me, and I want to make things easier for you, if I can, but it seems I can't.'

'You have helped me,' said Heather, 'you really have. More information always helps in processing things.'

'Well, don't make me regret giving you the information. Don't start any amateur sleuthing, right?' He looked and sounded stern now, almost fierce.

'Right,' she said. She could see that it would not be comfortable to be on the wrong side of DI John Kelly, not good to make an enemy of him.

'I must get back,' he said, his tone softer again. He gulped down his coffee. 'Too much coffee. Not good for the nerves, I know. You take care.'

He stood up to leave and touched her shoulder, and his touch sent an electric shock through her body, leaving her stunned for a few seconds. And then he was gone. His biro was on the table. She put it in her bag.

10

Heather phoned Max that evening. She was at home, sitting in her favourite armchair, with her feet up on the coffee table.

Max sounded tired. She thanked him for giving her the name of the pub where she might find the DI and explained that she'd found him, but it had been difficult to talk there, and they'd met again in a café. She told him what John had said about the forensic evidence in the flat and Phoebe's injuries.

'Oh, and they did some house-to-house enquiries,' she said, 'and didn't come up with any potential witnesses.'

'There was at least one witness,' said Max.

'Was there? Who? Do you mean someone who was with Phoebe when she fell?'

'I mean presumably someone found her and called the emergency services.'

'Oh, hell,' said Heather. 'Why didn't I think of that when I was with John? I could've asked him. Damn!'

'It's John, now, is it?' asked Max. 'Did you two hit it off, then?'

'I don't know about hit it off. He was very friendly and helpful. I like him. For a cop, he seems OK. He did warn me off what he called amateur sleuthing in no uncertain terms.'

'Good,' said Max. 'Perhaps you should take notice of him.'

'Max, it was you who said go for it in the first place, if you remember. And you didn't say that when I was round at your place recently.'

'Nah, but I've been thinking about it,' he said. 'I worry about you and what you might be getting into. Just a sec.' Max started coughing and it sounded as if he couldn't stop, and then she heard him drinking something and the cough subsided.

'You worry about me?' said Heather. 'Well, I worry about you. What are you drinking?'

'Water, hen. Just water.'

'A likely story. Have you seen a doctor about that cough?'

'Emphysema, they reckon.'

'Max, that's serious. You really need to stop smoking, and that means everything, not just tobacco.'

'Yeah, I'm gonna give it a go, if only to stop folk nagging me.'

'Make sure you do. You're stubborn enough, if you set your mind to it.'

'Thanks. Keep in touch about this investigation of yours, won't you?'

Heather felt churned up when she came off the phone. Max was her mentor and he made her feel safe, and now there was a possibility she could lose him. She hoped he wanted to quit smoking; if he wanted to, there was a good chance he could do it. But she wondered about his motivation, his will to go on. He seemed demoralised by the pain and mobility problems he was experiencing from the rheumatoid arthritis, and now he had lung disease as well.

The conversation with Max had started her thinking about her father. She hadn't seen him since his seventy-third birthday in March. James Delaney was another one who smoked and drank too much, and she was surprised he'd lived this long. She looked at her watch. Nine thirty. Not too late to call him. She quickly made a cup of tea and then called his landline, as he wasn't keen on his mobile. He took a while to answer. She imagined him snoozing in front of the television and waking with a start.

She could tell from his voice when he answered that he "had drink taken".

'Hello, Dad.'

'Is it yourself, Heather? Lovely to hear you. Just let me turn the television down.'

She could hear his uneven slippered footsteps on the carpet and some muttering as he looked for the remote. The television silenced, he returned to the phone.

'I was just dozing there,' he said. 'Nearly jumped out of my skin when the phone went.'

'Sorry I startled you. I was thinking about you and wanted to see if you're OK.'

'I'm fine, love.'

'Not at the pub tonight, then. Obviously!'

'I don't go every night, these days,' he said. 'Can't afford to. One of my friends I used to drink with died a couple of weeks ago. Ron. You remember him?'

'I think I met him, yes.'

'Well, he had a heart attack and died.'

'Oh, I'm sorry.'

'So, I was at the funeral last Thursday. Good turnout. Ron was the second one of us to go this year. Colm died in June. Pancreatic cancer.'

'I'm so sorry, Dad. It's very sad for you.'

'Well, they say when you get to a certain age your friends start dying off and it's all funerals then, and no weddings. Perhaps I'll be the next one to go.'

'Don't say that. Are you looking after yourself? Are you eating three meals a day?'

'Yes, I am. No need to worry on that score.'

'Tell me what you've eaten today. Humour me.'

'Now you're asking. I had porridge for breakfast, that's right. Probably soup at lunchtime. This evening I had one of those shepherd's pies you put in the oven. Convenience meal.'

Heather was doubtful about the "probably soup" at lunchtime.

'Do you have convenience meals every night?'

'A couple of days a week I have lunch in the pub. They do good home-cooked food at The Coach and Horses.'

'That's good.'

'Now, tell me about you,' he said. 'What's happening?'

'I'm still working as a therapist,' she said. 'There's no shortage of people with problems who want someone to talk to about them.'

'Isn't it depressing, listening to people's problems all day?'

'Not usually,' she said. 'People are interesting and

sometimes, just sometimes, I can help.' *It's not my clients who are depressing, as a rule,* she thought, *it's stubborn old men who won't look after themselves.*

'Now, I could do with a wedding, what with all these funerals. Is there a young man who is a likely candidate at the moment?'

'Sorry, Dad, I can't oblige. But I could come and see you for Christmas, if you'd like me to.'

'That would be grand, Heather, grand.'

She felt a bit down after the call, but her father was alive, indoors and was eating something, at least. And it seemed she'd made her plans for Christmas. She decided to watch television to take her mind off it all and found an episode of *Morse*. Chief Inspector Morse was another stubborn old man, but it was not the devastating final episode, so she decided to enjoy his detective work and the operatic soundtrack.

It turned out she wouldn't have to wait long to see DI John Kelly again. He left her a message asking her to call him. She thought he must have remembered something she might want to know. In fact, he wanted to ask her out. He had two tickets for *Carmen* at the Royal Opera House and wondered if she would like to come with him. She said yes immediately.

She wore a long patterned skirt from Monsoon, ankle boots with heels, a silky top, a swagger coat she'd found stowed away in a suitcase under her bed, dangly earrings, eye make-up, lipstick and her favourite perfume, Chanel No 5. She arrived at Covent Garden station and made her way up in the lift with the rest of the evening crowds.

She walked over the cobbles, holding her coat closed with one hand, her other hand on her bag, its strap across her body for security. She felt nervous, like a young girl going to a ball, and the colonnaded façade of the Royal Opera House rose before her like a palace. People were entering the building through the sets of double doors. Inside, the foyer was so gloriously huge that the people didn't fill the space, but were dwarfed, like tiny motionless cutouts on an architect's model. The décor was marble, wood, yellow lights, and a staircase swept up ahead of her and on the floor above, to the left and right.

John was standing at the bottom of the staircase. He was handsome tonight in a black suit, white shirt and dark tie. It was the first time she'd seen him clean-shaven, without a day or two of stubble. He reminded her of her father when he was scrubbed up and in his Sunday best; both were medium height, with striking dark eyes and a confident bearing. He smiled when he saw her. She wondered whether to kiss him on the cheek but felt shy and didn't.

'I could have booked us a table in one of the restaurants for before the performance,' he said. 'Sorry, I've been snowed under with work, and I didn't think of it till now. I hope you're not starving.'

'No, I've eaten something,' she said.

'We can eat afterwards,' he said, 'if you want to.'

'Yes, that would be good.'

He produced two tickets from his inside pocket.

'At least I've remembered these,' he said. 'Do you want to leave your coat in the cloakroom?'

'No, thanks, I'll keep it with me.'

'You look very nice,' he said.

'So do you.'

He asked if she would like a drink of anything. She declined and excused herself to find the ladies' toilet. It was grand and spotlessly clean, with hand driers and paper towels, tissues and hand cream supplied.

When she found John again, he'd bought her a glossy souvenir programme, which she accepted with thanks. They ascended the stairs to find their seats. Heather had only been there once before, to see *Otello*. When they entered the auditorium, she was thrilled again with the gold, the light and the acres of red plush. They were not quite in the gods, they were in an upper circle, not far from the front. Below, the stage was still curtained, and members of the orchestra were taking their seats and starting to tune up. She took off her coat and laid it across her knees. She was pleased to have the programme to look at as they waited. She told John that last time she was here, her seat had been so high up, she'd felt giddy if she stood and looked down. The theatre was filling up, the orchestra made its cacophony of tuning up sounds. The announcement came for ten minutes to curtain up.

Heather leant towards John. 'Thank you so much for inviting me,' she said. 'It really is thrilling. I'd forgotten.'

He smiled again. She noticed his hands as he turned off his mobile phone. They were capable, sensitive hands. She turned off her own phone.

The five-minute announcement came, and the two-minute, and then the orchestra began to play, the curtains slid back, and the stage was full of people and colour and movement, and a surging chorus of beautiful voices.

It was a three-hour performance with an interval of thirty minutes. At the interval, they decided to have ice cream, rather than queue for drinks. Eating ice cream out of a tub made Heather feel she was a child being given a treat on an outing. She told John and he agreed, saying he could remember having a tub of ice cream at the pictures when he was a child.

At the end of the show, after the cast had come out three times for curtain calls and the curtains had finally swung closed, Heather experienced a rare sense of her spirit being uplifted, a feeling of excitement and calmness at the same time. She didn't want to move from her seat, but everyone else was standing up, putting on coats, making their way to the exits.

'Shall we head off?' said John.

They joined the crowds making slow progress down the stairs. It took a while to get down to the foyer, and then they were out in the cold air on the piazza.

'Would you like something to eat?' asked John.

Heather shook her head. 'I'm not really that hungry, thanks.'

'Nor me,' he said. 'Let's get a drink.'

They walked to the other side of the piazza and entered a pub. John had his hand on Heather's back as they walked in and she decided she liked the feeling of it being there, despite the connotations of proprietorship; it felt protective. She asked him for a ginger ale and sat down at a table. John bought himself a pint of bitter. He didn't ask about the fact that she always went for non-alcoholic drinks, but she decided to tell him anyway that she used to drink too much and decided to stop altogether.

'It's probably a good idea,' he said. 'I feel under pressure to drink a lot with my colleagues and there have been times when I've definitely felt I was overdoing it and I've cut back for a while.'

'If you can control it, that's good,' she said. 'I don't think I can, so it's easier not to drink at all.'

She thanked him again for inviting her.

'Thank you for accepting,' said John. 'I'm quite jaded these days, and I enjoyed your enthusiasm.'

Sitting in that pub, he looked more relaxed than she'd seen him before, more mellow.

'I'm glad it was *Carmen*,' she said, 'because I can actually recognise some of it. What's the name of her aria?' She turned the pages of the programme. 'Yes, "*Habanera, L'amour est un oiseau rebelle*". It's beautiful.'

They talked about the performance, which they agreed had been excellent, and about the demands of work making it difficult to do the things you enjoy, and how you have to make the time and the effort or you can end up just working and sleeping.

Heather was beginning to come down from her uplifted state, and was aware that she wanted to ask John something about the Phoebe case and this might be her only chance, but she felt uncomfortable about asking, and didn't want to annoy him, or spoil their rapport. She decided to ask him anyway.

'I'm sorry, John,' she said. 'I don't want to harp on about my client who died when I feel, I hope, we're getting on quite well, but I want to ask you something about that case.'

'OK,' he said.

'You were so helpful, giving me all that information

when we met in the café, but afterwards something occurred to me, something that was missing from the narrative.'

John nodded and she felt encouraged to continue.

'You said there were no witnesses when Phoebe fell, but did someone call an ambulance?'

'Ah! It was the man from the off-licence on the corner, if I remember rightly. He heard something and went out to investigate.'

Heather was taken aback by this piece of information. She wasn't sure what she'd been expecting, but it wasn't this. She stared at John's face, looking for something more.

'No-one else was around?' she asked.

'Not to my knowledge,' said John.

She felt it was not advisable to pursue it further, not if she wanted to remain in his good books.

'Well, thank you, and sorry again for raising it this evening.'

When they had finished their drinks, John proposed getting a black cab back to West London. Heather said she thought this was terrifically extravagant, but he said it was on him and not to worry about it, so they walked to Long Acre and John hailed a cab. It felt romantic, sitting next to John in that dark, leather-lined space, speeding through the lights and sounds of the city. They were both quiet for most of the journey and then, as the cab left the A4 at the Chiswick turn-off, Heather turned to John and he leant towards her and kissed her. It was not a long, lingering kiss; it felt like a kind of signal.

'I'll call you, shall I?' he said.

'Yes, please.'

Heather moved forward in her seat and gave

instructions to the driver, and then she was climbing out of the cab in front of her house. She leant into the cab and said goodnight to John. He continued to look at her face as she slammed the heavy door and stood back on the pavement to wave him off.

She allowed herself to bask in a romantic glow for the rest of the evening. She ironed an outfit and packed her work bag ready for the next day. She made cocoa, changed into her pyjamas and sat drinking the cocoa in the sitting room with just one small lamp shining in a corner. This was the anticipatory stage of the relationship, full of promise, not yet complicated – or not much – and she wanted to savour it. She wouldn't think about the complications yet. She thought about the spirited performance they had seen that evening, and the beautiful music. Mostly she thought about John, standing at the foot of the stairs in his suit, his hand on her back as they entered the pub, the brief kiss, his face through the taxi window.

In the morning, the rosy glow and sense of anticipation were still there and when she arrived at work, she greeted the receptionist and the centre manager, Vicki, who was passing through reception, with more bonhomie than usual. She was sure they both gave her a second glance. Empathy and warmth came easily when she was with her clients and her mind was clear, her insights sharp. Late morning, she had a text from John, thanking her for the evening and saying he would call her when pressure of work eased up. She smiled to herself, thinking of those television cops failing to turn up for a date or event because of work, or called to a murder scene just as dinner was served.

11

The next day Phoebe was in her head again from the moment she woke. She thought about John's revelation that it was a shopkeeper who called the ambulance for Phoebe. What could she do with this information? There was nothing for it but to visit the shopkeeper and see what she could find out from him. She didn't want complications with John over this. Maybe she just wouldn't tell him she was continuing to investigate. But keeping it from him could cause complications as well. She was at the therapy centre again today, with a busy caseload. It was good to be busy, but as she sat with her clients, she noticed that she was not as focused as the day before, her mind was not as clear. She was distracted occasionally and at times felt impatient. Writing up her notes about David, she felt like writing that he was "whining again". How could she sustain this work when she was so obsessed with Phoebe and her death? Maybe she would have to talk to Val about it at her next supervision, if she wanted to keep her job. For now, all she wanted to do was follow up on what John had told her. She'd found a new addiction and needed her fix.

After work she took a detour on her way home. The clocks had gone back at the end of October, and it was dark at that time. Would it have been better to go in daylight? Maybe, but she was impatient to visit the shopkeeper and didn't want to wait for the weekend.

She turned into the street where Phoebe had lived and felt a fluttering in her stomach. It was the first time she'd visited Phoebe's home ground and the scene of her death. She'd looked many times at the address and found it on the map but had avoided coming here. Now she had a specific task to do, a mission. John would not be happy about what she was doing, she knew that, but she felt compelled to do it.

It was a quiet tree-lined side street, well-lit with streetlamps, red-brick mansion blocks on both sides with grass and railings at the front. Cars were parked along both sides of the street. On the side where she was walking, the mansion blocks gave way to tall terraced houses. Rowan trees were planted at intervals, their orange berries scattered over the pavement. She remembered something about rowans warding off evil spirits. It hadn't worked for Phoebe.

She arrived outside the housing association block, Edith Court. It was set back a few feet from the pavement, its walls pinkish brick, paler than the red brick of the mansion blocks, with a paved area between the front doors of the ground-floor flats and the pavement. Heather looked up. There were five floors, and Phoebe had lived on the fourth. The balconies had painted metal railings and on some she could make out the dark shapes of plant pots, a bicycle, washing on a line. She didn't know which had been Phoebe's balcony.

She stood outside the entrance, a door with a glass panel, keypad at the side to call the resident you wanted to visit. Approaching the glass, she could see, inside, a red-tiled floor, a lift and a staircase. How many times had Martin hovered out here? How many times had he keyed in Phoebe's number, waited for her voice and been let in, or, later in the relationship, been turned away?

Heather sighed and moved away from the door. Gripping her work bag, she continued to walk along the street. There was a junction a few yards away. Cars and buses passed the end of the street in both directions. And on the corner was the shop, the off-licence John had mentioned. Coming alongside the shop window, she could see that it was a general store as well, selling groceries, confectionery, household goods. She pushed open the door and a bell jangled loudly.

It was only when she was inside the shop that Heather realised how cold it was outside. An electric heater was suspended from the ceiling in the back corner, giving the shop its welcoming warmth. The counter was across the far end of the shop and an elderly Asian man was behind it, serving a woman who was buying cat litter and a bottle of wine. She was telling him about taking her cat to the vet; he nodded and expressed sympathy and smiled at the cat's happy outcome. Heather looked at a display of cleaning materials and waited. The woman finished her transaction and walked towards the door with her purchases, wrapped up in coat, scarf and bobble hat and looking cheerful after her exchange with the shopkeeper. Heather went to one of the fridges, took out a small bottle of Evian water and made her way to the counter.

'Just that, dear?'

'Yes, thank you,' said Heather.

She took her purse from her bag and paid him for the water. He opened his till and gave her change. He had a kind face and a gentle, courteous manner. She was reluctant to remind him of something that was bound to be a distressing memory.

'Is there something else?' he asked.

'Yes, actually, I want to ask you about something that happened in the street out there in the summer.'

'How can I help?'

'Three months ago, a young woman fell to her death from one of the balconies in Edith Court, just a few yards away from here. I wonder, do you remember anything about that?'

'Are you with the police?' he asked. He looked wary. 'I did answer their questions at the time.'

'No, I worked with Phoebe, the young woman who died, I was quite close to her, and I'm trying to understand what happened. I'm so sorry to ask you to think back to such a distressing incident, but anything you can tell me…'

'Of course, I'll tell you,' he said. 'It was a hot evening. My wife had come down and I left her behind the counter and went to the door to get some air. As I stepped outside, I heard, I remember it clearly, a dull thud of something heavy hitting the ground. It was a terrible sound. I hurried along and saw the young lady lying there and I straight away called an ambulance and the police on my mobile. I'm sorry for your loss, dear. There was nothing I could do for her but call for the ambulance.'

It must have been the closeness of the scene of Phoebe's death, combined with the comforting warmth of the shop and the kindness of the shopkeeper. Heather felt grief well up in her chest and tears spring to her eyes; she was aware that this was the first time since Phoebe died that she had felt like this and she wanted to give way to it and cry, even if once she started, she wouldn't be able to stop. The shopkeeper was at her side offering her a pack of tissues. He was shorter than he appeared to be when he was behind the counter.

'I can get a chair for you, some water,' he was saying. 'I know how upsetting it is for you.'

'No need, I have some, thank you,' she said. 'I'll be OK in a minute.'

She took a tissue from her bag and wiped her eyes and blew her nose. She unscrewed the bottle of water and took a drink.

'You're very kind,' she said. 'Thank you for calling for help for Phoebe.'

He spread his hands. 'It was too late and I'm sorry for that.'

A man of about fifty came into the shop and approached the counter with some cans of lager. Heather stood to one side whilst the shopkeeper served him, and a young man in a suit who bought a bottle of wine. When they had both left, she thought she'd better finish asking her questions before any more customers came in.

'My name is Heather,' she said. 'Can I ask, what's your name?'

'I'm Wahid,' he said.

'Thank you, Wahid, for talking to me and being so kind.

I have just one more thing to ask. Was anyone else around that evening who saw what happened or saw the body?'

'There was just a young man. I was telling my wife what had happened, and he came into the shop, very agitated, said he was passing and saw the young lady there and had no credit on his phone to call an ambulance, so I told him I had called them.'

'Do you remember what he looked like?'

'White, long dark hair. He'd been in the shop a couple of times before.'

'Really? Did you tell the police about him?'

'I did,' he said, 'and they said I should have asked him to wait because he was a witness, but I didn't think at the time, and he left.'

'He was in a hurry to leave, was he?'

Wahid shrugged. 'He was shaken up. He didn't want to hang around, I suppose. I went back outside then to wait for the ambulance to come.'

'I expect more people came out when the ambulance arrived, did they? They usually do.'

'Oh, yes, a little crowd gathered, but no-one knew anything, the police said. No-one ever knows anything.'

A group of young people entered the shop, three men and a woman, laughing and joking and discussing how much beer and wine to buy. Heather decided it was time to leave.

'Thank you so much for your help, Wahid,' she said.

He reached over the counter, offered his hand to her and she shook it. She might easily have forgotten her work bag, but she almost tripped over it. She picked it up, slid her bottle of water into it and left the shop.

Outside, the cold air hit her. She put her collar up and turned into the road where she'd seen the buses. She didn't want to walk back past Phoebe's block. The emotion that had come over her in the shop still lingered and she wanted to get home.

12

Late November. Heather raked leaves from her lawn and wondered if and when John would phone her. She also wondered whether to tell him she'd seen the shopkeeper, Wahid, and whether to ask him why he hadn't mentioned the young man who had come into the shop just after Wahid had called the ambulance for Phoebe. She knew it was a bad idea, at this stage anyway, to confront Martin and ask him if he was the young man in the shop. She was impatient to do something, but felt she had to keep plodding on, going to work, coming home, waiting for John's call, going over the notes from her sessions with Phoebe and finding nothing new or helpful. She had a supervision with Val and didn't mention her impatience and difficulty focusing; most of the time she was functioning well enough. In terms of her investigation, she had reached an impasse.

In December, it started to be very cold. It was dark in the mornings and when it got light and she opened the curtains at the back, there was frost on the grass and fog obscured the trees at the end of her garden and the houses beyond. It was on one of these cold mornings that she received a call from the hospital. She had just arrived at work and was hanging up her coat. The caller was a staff nurse on the respiratory ward. Max had been admitted with breathing difficulties and when asked if he wanted them to call anyone, he had asked for her. She said she would come and see him after work.

Max was in a side ward with five other patients, in the bed nearest the door to the corridor and the nurses' station. He was lying with his eyes closed and an oxygen mask over his mouth and nose. He looked old and his skin had a greyish tinge. His breathing was laboured. Heather pulled up a chair and sat near the head of the bed.

He opened his eyes, lowered the oxygen mask.

'Hello, hen. Thanks for coming.' His voice was weak, and he struggled for breath.

'I brought you *The Guardian* and some juice,' she said, and placed both on the bedside cabinet.

'No grapes?'

'I didn't think you'd want them.'

'Nah, I wouldn't. Thanks.' He replaced the mask over his face.

'The nurse said you collapsed in the street,' she said. 'Do they know at work?'

He nodded.

'I'm glad you asked the nurse to call me. Shall I get in touch with your daughter for you? Elizabeth, isn't it?'

He shook his head, lowered the mask again. 'No. I don't want her bothered.'

Heather knew Elizabeth lived in Scotland, somewhere near Stirling, had a full-time job and two children.

'Oh, Max, she'd want to know.'

'I'll not be in here long,' he said.

'Give me her number, just in case. Please.'

'You think I might peg out.'

'No, I don't. I'd want to know if my dad was ill and in hospital, that's all.'

His pig-headedness might just be what pulls him through this, she thought. If he could use it to quit smoking, he might stand a chance of living for a few more years. At least he hadn't asked her to take him outside for a smoke. She supposed he was too weak.

He pulled up the sleeve of his gown and showed her a clear plaster on his upper arm.

'Nicotine patch,' he said, through the mask.

'You must've read my mind,' she said. 'You can stop doing that, right now. Good about the patch.' She leant in closer and whispered, 'How's the company in here?'

'Old and ill,' he said.

One of the other patients was being attended to by a nurse and a health-care assistant, who drew the curtain around him. The others appeared to be sleeping.

Max wanted to know how things were going so she told him, in a hushed voice, about going to the opera with John, her visit to the off-licence, the young man who might have been Martin and her sense of coming to a standstill.

He said something and she didn't catch it.

He lowered the mask. 'Tread carefully,' he said. 'Keep John onside.'

'I'll certainly try to.'

She asked if he wanted her to bring him anything and he asked for a toothbrush, shaving kit, clean clothes. He gave her the keys to his flat and eventually gave her his daughter's number. She was not to call Elizabeth without his say so.

Heather spoke to one of the nurses before leaving. She explained that no, she was not a relative, but his daughter lived in Scotland, and she was going to contact her and wanted to be able to explain the situation. The nurse said it was an exacerbation of COPD.

'Chronic obstructive pulmonary disease,' said the nurse. 'Chronic bronchitis and emphysema. It can flair up like this and we call that an exacerbation. The condition is progressive, but it can be slowed down if he stops smoking. The doctor has told him.'

She said that there should be an improvement within a few days and then he would be able to go home. He would be provided with a rescue pack of antibiotics and steroid tablets in case of a flare up in the future.

Heather thanked the nurse and picked up a leaflet about COPD from a rack in the corridor.

She went straight from the hospital to Max's flat. His sitting room was dustier and more cluttered, and the carpet was even messier than when she had last been there. His bedroom smelled stale, the bed a tangle of grubby sheets, the laundry basket was overflowing and there was a pile of crumpled clothes on a chair. She would come back and tidy up and do his washing before he was discharged from hospital. She found a pair of trousers, shirt, jumper and jacket in the wardrobe and clean underwear and socks in the chest of drawers. In the bathroom, as she expected, the sink and bath were grimy, and she decided to clean them straight away; there was a cloth and some cream cleaner.

She sprayed cleaner into the toilet bowl. The floor she would leave for now. There was an old metal razor on the sink. She would buy him some disposable razors, a toothbrush and paste on the way to the hospital the next day. Before leaving, she peeped into the kitchen and saw that some dirty dishes had been left and the surfaces and floor needed cleaning.

Heather called Elizabeth anyway. Elizabeth was shocked as she didn't know her father had lung disease, only about the arthritis. Heather told her the staff had said Max was responding to treatment and would be discharged in a few days. She would keep her informed about how things were going. Elizabeth said she would come down to London, but as he was out of danger, she would arrange to come once Max was at home. She needed to make arrangements. She thanked Heather for letting her know and for visiting her father in hospital. She sounded distressed.

'It's awfully difficult that he's so far away,' Elizabeth said. 'My mum's been poorly, and I've had to go to hospital appointments with her. I thought Dad was managing OK.'

Heather sympathised and explained that her own father was some distance away, though not as far as Max was from Elizabeth. She gave Elizabeth the hospital number and ward details.

Heather visited Max every evening after work. He was given a discharge date of the following Monday, so on Saturday she returned to his flat and did his laundry, tidied up, dusted, cleaned. Whilst she was there, John called. She had to peel off rubber gloves to answer the phone. He invited her out that evening, so she suggested a time that would allow her to visit Max first. When she had finished her chores, she hurried home and showered and changed and put on some make-up.

That evening, she gave Max his keys back and told him she had contacted Elizabeth. He accepted it with a shrug.

'She called me this morning,' he said. 'I'd have told her myself once I got out of here.'

They met in a Turkish restaurant. John was wearing a black overcoat and was unshaven again. Heather thought he looked attractively disreputable. He smiled when he saw her. A waiter showed them to a table at the side, took their coats and returned to light the candle on the table.

Heather told John she'd been visiting an old friend in hospital.

'You might know him. He knows you. Max Gallagher? He's a private investigator.'

'Oh, yes, Max. How is he?'

Heather told him what had happened to Max and that his daughter was in Scotland, so she had stepped in.

They ordered drinks – a beer for John and tap water for Heather.

'How come you're mixed up with Max?' he asked.

'I had a temp job at the agency in the distant past. We used to drink together. Now he drinks and I watch. His daughter is coming down, hopefully.'

John was quiet for a few minutes, studying the menu and then he looked up at Heather.

'Did you ask him to look into your client's death?' he asked.

'Oh, no. We're friends.'

John was looking at her in the intent way she'd noticed when they first met, his brown eyes alert and penetrating. He nodded and turned his attention back to the menu.

They ordered meze. To follow, John ordered lamb shish, and Heather chose sea bass.

'I've been thinking, I don't know anything about you,' said Heather. 'I know what your job is and that you like strong coffee and opera and that's about it.'

'I like jazz as well, and films, and I like food, especially Turkish and Indian. I work long hours, and I like to get results. What do you want to know?'

'You're not married, are you?'

'Not anymore. I was married for twelve years to Claire, and we have two children, a boy and a girl. I see the children as often as I can. Does that help?'

'Yes, thank you.'

The meze arrived and they shared the food, both taking a bit of each starter. They agreed the cheese and spinach pastries were particularly good. When they'd finished they sat back as the waiter cleared the table. John ordered another beer.

'What about you?' he said. 'Any husbands or children?'

'I was married, only briefly, when I was very young,' she said. 'I haven't any children, sadly.'

'It's not too late, is it?'

Heather thought for a moment. 'It might still be biologically possible,' she said, 'but it may be too late mentally. I don't know.'

The waiter brought the main courses, served on very large plates with salad and rice. They stopped talking for a while and concentrated on the food.

'Will you spend Christmas with your children?' said Heather.

'I hope so, yes. What about you? What are your Christmas plans?'

'I'm going to see my dad in Nottingham.'

'Do you get on with your dad?'

Heather put down her knife and fork. 'He's charming and funny, but he drinks too much and I'm sure he's not looking after himself properly,' she said. 'That's one reason I'm going; he's convincing on the phone, but I want to see for myself.' She returned to eating her fish, carefully separating the white flesh from the bones. 'I'm used to fillets from the supermarket with no eyes,' she said. 'It's delicious, though.'

She liked the way John looked in the candlelight, his shoulders relaxed, the tension gone from his face, his brown eyes mellow. She breathed a sigh of relief and pleasure.

He smiled at her. 'It's good to see you again,' he said. 'I'm sorry I haven't been in touch before, and it was such short notice. I've been thinking about you.'

'That's good,' she said.

He reached across the table and touched the back of her hand. She turned her hand over and clasped his. After a moment, they both withdrew their hands, but their eyes held each other's for a moment longer. She'd seen that intense look in a man's eyes before and felt a thrill go through her.

She didn't want to risk telling him she'd been to the shop near Phoebe's flat or asking him anything about the case. Not now.

Nor did she think it was a good time to talk about the case when they left the restaurant and took a taxi to her house. This time, John came into the house and stayed the night with her.

13

Heather was eating a sandwich at the kitchen table at Number 27 and Mrs Bird, who owned the house, was sitting next to her with a mug of tea. Mrs Bird was a feisty elderly woman. She lived mainly upstairs, but her kitchen was on the ground floor, at the back of the house. Her GP son had suggested that she rent the downstairs rooms to therapists. He said it would be less demanding and risky than having tenants or lodgers. The son had a practice in Plymouth and must have thought that, as he couldn't be around, a couple of therapists would do to look out for his old mum. It was a good arrangement, as long as Mrs Bird could still manage the stairs. She'd told Heather that one of her friends who lived alone had died and her body hadn't been found for three days. She didn't want this to happen to her. 'I'm all right as long as I don't die on a Saturday morning, aren't I?' she'd said, with a bright laugh.

'It's nice to sit and chat with you, dear,' said Mrs Bird. 'It breaks up my day. When I've done my shopping in the morning, the day can be long and there's nothing on the television until *Countdown* in the afternoon.'

'Have you thought about going shopping later in the day?' said Heather. 'You could call in for a coffee or a cup of tea in a café.'

'Oh, no, I like to get it done early. And I wouldn't go to a café. It would be a waste of money when I've got plenty of tea and coffee here. Now, tell me, dear, are you busy seeing patients? I don't hear the bell so often these days.'

'My clients keep me busy enough,' said Heather. 'I'd better get back to it.'

'It's bitterly cold today,' said Mrs Bird. 'Make sure you wrap up when you go out.'

Heather made tea and took it to her consulting room. She didn't have enough clients, and it was disconcerting that Mrs Bird had picked this up. She hadn't been making much of an effort to build up her private practice; she'd been preoccupied with trying to process and understand Phoebe's death and, recently, with Max being ill, and the relationship with John Kelly. She often wondered about the wisdom of having a relationship with John. When she was with him it felt right; indeed, it felt wonderful, but a policeman? What's more, the policeman who had been investigating Phoebe's death and had handed the case to the coroner? She'd decided not to tell him she'd been to Wahid's shop, so she was keeping something from him, and she would always wonder if he knew about the young man who was in the shop on the night Phoebe died and didn't tell her. Could she afford to keep paying for the room here at Number 27? Did Mrs Bird hear the doorbell more often on the days when the other therapist was here on the other days of the week? Probably, but she mustn't dwell on that. Max was at home now and Elizabeth had been down from Scotland to see him. Heather would phone him later to see how things were going. She had a client coming at four o'clock. She made some phone calls and there was still time to spare. She would look through some Phoebe sessions and think about how to proceed with the investigation. She pulled the file out of her bag and found the session in June she wanted to look at:

Phoebe said, 'Sometimes I don't want to be here. I don't want to be in this world. I'm not saying I'll kill myself. It's just all too much.'

Long pauses, waiting for her, had to prompt her to say more.

Said she drags herself out of bed, makes herself shower and have breakfast, feeling sick, having to help people in distress at work, "puts on a face".

Re Martin – he doesn't call her at work now but after work "it starts". She wants to go home and have peace, but he calls or she is expecting him to call. If she doesn't answer, he might come round and ring her intercom.

What would she like to happen?

'I want him to leave me alone.'

What could she do about it?

She said she could move away, but why should she?

I agreed, why should she? I said one option was to report him to the police for stalking her.

She said she couldn't do that to him. Maybe Alan could scare him off. She laughed.

I asked why this was funny.

She said she was joking and wouldn't really ask Alan to do that.

Talked about taking time off work – feelings, consequences, how to manage.

Will she ask Alan for help?

Low mood – monitor. Help needed re alcohol?

There were sessions closer to the time of her death where Phoebe was more positive, her mood was improved, and she was growing more confident in her work. She seemed to reach an accommodation with Martin, seeing him sometimes, keeping him at bay most of the time. It didn't sound satisfactory, and Heather had wondered what would happen if Phoebe met someone else. This was never fully explored in the sessions and when Heather asked about Alan, Phoebe said she hadn't involved him.

The doorbell rang at five to four. She put away the Phoebe file, adjusted the chairs and went to open the door for her client.

In the evening she called Max. He sounded a lot better, as if his breathing was easier.

'How did it go with Elizabeth?' she asked.

'She was fussing over me something terrible,' he said. 'She wants me to move up to Scotland so she can fuss over me on a regular basis.'

This hit Heather like a bombshell. She took a deep breath. How would she manage without Max if he moved away?

'What about your job?' she said.

'I'd have to give up work,' he said. 'Retire to the

knacker's yard. I've told her no way. She wants to organise a sheltered flat for me. Fuck that.'

The following evening, she went round to see him with an Indian takeaway. When he opened the door she was pleased to see that, although he was stooping a bit, he had a healthier colour, was clean shaven and was dressed in an ironed shirt and jeans. The flat was still tidy, following her ministrations and those of Elizabeth, and the heating was on. He was sometimes mean with the heating. She kissed him on both cheeks and put the bag of food on a mat on the table.

'What did you get?' asked Max.

'Vindaloo for you, of course,' she said.

'Just the job.'

She fetched plates, cutlery and glasses of water and they sat at the table. She prised the tops off the foil containers, releasing a delicious aroma of cumin, coriander and garlic. The dish with thick brown gravy and pieces of potato was obviously the vindaloo and the reddish one with peppers was the jalfrezi. They served themselves from the containers.

Max was still signed off from work. Heather asked how he passed the time, and he said he watched the BBC news channel, and it was a chance to go online and catch up with the latest gen on Rangers; he'd followed the financial collapse and subsequent misfortunes of that football club with great glee. He was pleased to be out of hospital.

'The staff were great,' he said, 'but I don't want to end up back in there. It's deadly.'

Heather took a naan bread from a bag and tore off

a piece. 'Have you thought any more about moving to Scotland?'

'Yes. I'm not going,' he said. 'What would I do, for God's sake? I'd end up in the pub. I'd be one of those old codgers sitting there all day with a half and half, watching football and racing on the television, popping out to the bookie's and going home to a heated-up pie or a tin of soup. Nah. The only thing I miss is square sausages and I can live without them.'

'Is that really all you miss?'

'Well, I suppose the air and the hills, and not living amongst the English has its attractions.'

She smiled. 'What about Elizabeth and your grandchildren?'

'Them as well. Are you trying to persuade me to piss off to Scotland?'

'No,' said Heather. 'I want you here, so I can pick your brains and cry on your shoulder. I need your help looking into Phoebe's death. But I want what's best for you and it may be best to be near your family now.'

'What, now that I'm sick and decrepit, you mean?'

'You're looking a lot better, and I hope you stay well, but this COPD won't go away. You might need some care later and Elizabeth wants you near her so she can arrange help if needed and look out for you.'

'Sure, she's a good girl, but I know the score and I can look after myself. I haven't touched tobacco or weed since I got home. I don't need a sheltered flat or mollycoddling. I need to get back to work.'

He helped himself to more rice and vindaloo. Heather sipped water and ate a forkful of jalfrezi.

'You've made up your mind, then?' she said.
'Yep.'

Despite Max's protestations that he would be staying put, Heather suspected that Elizabeth would get her way, and she was right. He phoned Heather a week later and told her he had decided to go and would be staying with Elizabeth until his flat was ready in January. Heather felt sick with misery at this news but wished him well and promised to visit.

A week before Christmas, Max moved to Stirling. Elizabeth arranged for his furniture and possessions to be transported to Scotland for storage.

Heather felt bereft; she didn't know who she could talk to now. Maybe she could have long telephone conversations with Max once he was in his own place, and she could visit him in Stirling. But she felt her life had changed forever, for the worse.

She travelled up to Nottingham on the twenty-third of December. She went straight from the station to a supermarket and bought something for dinner that evening and, for Christmas Day, a chicken, packets of stuffing and bread sauce mix, a bag of sprouts, a small Christmas pudding. She would see what else her father needed and shop again the next day. She arrived at his flat, in a taxi, in the late afternoon. He had a one-bedroom flat on the ground floor in a sheltered block and Heather had booked the guest room for four nights. She rang the intercom, and he buzzed her in. He came down the corridor to meet her and took her case. He had on a green lambswool cardigan, a polo shirt, slacks and slippers and seemed shorter than she remembered.

'It's lovely to see you, darlin',' he said with a broad smile. When they reached the kitchen, he said, 'Will you have a cup of tea, or something stronger?'

'Tea, please, Dad. I don't drink anything stronger, if you remember.'

'Of course you don't. Sorry, love.'

He put the kettle on and got mugs ready whilst she put away the shopping. The fridge contained four cans of Guinness and not much else. To her surprise, the kitchen was clean and tidy.

The sitting room had a threadbare look, but the carpet had been hoovered and the surfaces dusted. A dozen or so Christmas cards were displayed on the sideboard and bookcase.

'No tree, Dad?'

'If you want a tree, love, we'll get a tree.'

''No, it's OK. Can I look at your cards?'

When they'd drunk the tea, Heather went to install herself in the guest room at the far end of the corridor. Her father had collected the key from the office, and he also gave her a key to his flat. She'd stayed in the guest room before. It had a single bed, wardrobe, chair, pink flowery décor and furnishings, and an en suite bathroom with walk-in shower. It was fine for four nights. She hung up her clothes and placed her books on the bedside table and her toiletries in the bathroom.

She let herself back into her father's flat.

'It's only me, Dad.'

'I thought it was. What a pleasure it is to have you here.'

'I've got oven fish and chips for dinner. Shall I get it started?'

She switched on the oven. It was electric, quite old and would take a while to heat up. She looked in the cupboards and found baked beans, spaghetti hoops, tinned soup, packets of soup, tinned fruit, Shreddies. The only coffee was instant.

They ate the fish and chips on their laps in front of the television, and the television stayed on all evening. When one of the soaps came on, he turned the sound right down.

'I can't stand this rubbish,' he said. 'How's your mother?'

'She's OK. I haven't spoken to her for a while.'

James Delaney was not in touch with his ex-wife; he had no time for her current partner, Phillip, and had described him as "a lily-livered lap dog". Heather would not disagree with her father's assessment.

'How are your friends in the pub?' she asked him.

'Fine. Apart from Ron, he died, I told you. Heart attack.'

'Do you know anyone else in this block?'

'They have get-togethers in that lounge, but I don't go.'

'Why not, Dad?'

'Phh! It's a load of old biddies from what I've seen. They play bingo, and they all bake cakes.'

'You like cake.'

'Yes, but it's a lot of vexation to put up with for a slice of Victoria sponge. It's not good for the blood pressure.'

His cheeks were ruddy, and his brown eyes were shining with pleasure.

'Oh, Dad. There might be some nice women amongst them. You could exercise your famous charm on them.'

He looked sidelong at her.

'There must be a few men in the block, as well,' she said.

'There's an ex-army type who's going doolally,' he said, 'and an ex-Tory councillor who thinks Margaret Thatcher was the bee's knees.'

'Oh dear. How about another cup of tea?'

Heather had tea and he had a can of Guinness.

'Who's this young man you're seeing now?' he asked.

'His name is John and he's a detective inspector in the police.'

'Jesus! You're sleeping with the enemy.'

Heather hadn't expected him to approve, but she knew he wouldn't let this information spoil the evening.

At about ten thirty, she kissed her father goodnight and went to her room to read. She wondered if he'd gone for the whisky once she'd left.

In the morning, she showered and dressed and headed for her father's flat for breakfast. She would buy a different cereal and some real coffee; she had bought him a cafetière for Christmas, partly to use herself when she visited. She let herself in and could hear a radio; it sounded like Radio 4.

'Morning, Dad.'

She went into the sitting room. He was in the chair he'd sat in the evening before, in his pyjamas, and it was clear to her that something was wrong because he looked listless and one side of his face had dropped.

'Dad!'

She ran over to him.

'Raise your arms, Dad. Speak to me.'

He looked at her but was unable to reply. She took her mobile from her bag and dialled 999. Whilst she waited for the ambulance, she pulled the alarm cord to alert the warden.

So Heather spent Christmas at her father's bedside in the hospital. He was in the stroke unit, paralysed on his left side. He could speak, but it was an effort and his speech was slurred. He looked frightened and was confused about where he was. Heather fed him his Christmas dinner with a spoon and wiped away the food that ran down his chin. During ward rounds, she waited in the corridor and asked for an update afterwards. He'd been brought to the unit quickly and the doctors were hopeful that, with physiotherapy, he would regain the use of his arm and leg. When the nurses came to bathe him, change him, she went to the café and had coffee, a tuna sandwich, crisps, chocolate cake. In those first few days, she was like an automaton, doing whatever was necessary; her feelings seemed to be on hold.

At night, she took a taxi to her father's flat, made tea, watched television and then went to the guest room to sleep. She cooked the chicken one evening, as she didn't want it to go to waste, and ate a few bits of the meat with bread and butter.

She phoned her brother, Anthony; he was away for Christmas and would come to the hospital on his return. She called her mother, Sonia, who sympathised but didn't show any inclination to visit. She phoned her father's brother in Ireland, Ray, and he would tell the other siblings and the cousins.

When her four nights in the guest room were up, she considered moving into the flat, but the warden said the guest room was still available, so she booked it for four more nights. Ray was coming over to visit his brother; he could stay in the flat.

On the fifth day, she went to the hospital in the morning as usual and when she arrived in the ward, she was shocked to find her father's bed empty.

'Where's my dad?' she asked a passing nurse, her heart pounding.

She thought he was dead. But he had been taken for a brain scan.

That evening, she called John and found herself crying over the phone, crying for the first time since her father's stroke.

Phoebe had often talked about her father, Tom, the journalist, who had died of lung cancer when she was fourteen years old. In her memory, he could do no wrong. He was handsome and good-humoured, playful and always patient. He had taken her to the fair, to the seaside, played crazy golf with her, told her stories, taken photographs of her. At home he was often closeted away in his study, writing. Her mother, Jean, she remembered as impatient, nagging her to get ready for school, lay the table, do her homework, get ready for bed. But Jean adored her husband, Phoebe said, and she softened in his presence. The three of them had holidays in Cornwall, Wales, and, later, Spain and Greece, and Phoebe had good memories of those times.

'*Are you angry with him for leaving you?*' Heather had asked her.

Phoebe looked indignant.

'*No,*' she said. '*I'm angry with her for not telling me he was ill for ages. And for clearing his study when I was away, and for taking up with Alan. I'm angry with her.*'

Now Heather had faced the possibility of losing her own father. It wasn't the same at all, as she was much older than Phoebe had been, and it looked as if James would recover. But she felt that maybe she had an inkling of what it might have been like for Phoebe to suffer that terrible loss at the beginning of adolescence. Just an inkling.

14

There were a few snowdrops in the shady parts of Heather's garden. She went for a walk in Chiswick House grounds and there were thousands of snowdrops there. New life, growing and flowering despite the cold ground and the dustings of snow in January. Heather's joy at seeing them was tinged with sadness. Phoebe would never see snowdrops again, or daffodils, or cherry blossom in March, bluebells in April.

The news was good about her father. He'd been discharged from hospital and was back in his flat. He could walk with a stick and had regained some use of his left arm. He had a care package which included physiotherapy, a personal alarm to wear around his neck and a carer coming in twice a day, and Heather had arranged for a cleaner to go in three times a week. She planned to go to Nottingham at least once a month. Fortunately, Anthony lived in Nottingham, and he would be able to take their father to most of his medical appointments.

Max had moved into his sheltered flat in Stirling and when Heather spoke to him on the phone he sounded resolutely cheerful about making a new life there. He told her about live music at the Tolbooth arts centre and taking his grandchildren to the cinema. She promised to arrange a trip to visit him in the spring. She was glad he was settling in but missed being able to see him whenever she wanted to.

Since returning to work in the New Year, she'd had a bit of trouble in relation to a client at the therapy centre. A young man she'd been seeing for a few weeks started asking her if they could see each other outside the sessions. He was a clean-cut young man, anxious and tense, and she'd sensed that he was relieved to be able to talk to her. Now he said he was in love with her and wanted to have a relationship with her. She explained about transference and how it was not uncommon to have such feelings towards a therapist, and that they could explore this in the sessions, but it would be inappropriate and unhelpful to meet outside. She felt uncomfortable about seeing the young man, whose name was Nick, as he persisted with his declarations, and she was looking forward to discussing it in supervision. But before the next supervision, the situation escalated.

At lunchtime, after she'd seen Nick in the morning, Heather went to the local Caffè Nero for a coffee and a toasted panini. She sat on a bench seat near the window with her coffee, took off her coat and scarf, took out her phone and was awaiting her food when Nick appeared next to her table, pulled out a chair opposite her and sat down. He must have waited around after the session and followed her to the café. She felt nervous and exposed.

'Hi,' he said. 'So this is where you hang out.'

'I sometimes come here,' she said. 'Not every day.'

The barista arrived at the table with Heather's panini and Nick asked her if he could have a flat white. She said he would need to come to the counter to pay. He followed her to the counter and looked back at Heather as he waited for his change and his coffee. Heather had lost her appetite; she had no wish to eat in front of him and decided to finish her coffee and take the panini back to the office. She felt irritation welling up at this interruption of her own time, and his obtuseness.

Nick returned to the table with his coffee.

'I hope you don't mind me joining you like this,' he said.

'Actually, I do mind,' she said. 'I have explained to you that we can only meet in our sessions in the centre. And this is my lunch hour.'

'Please eat your lunch,' he said. 'Don't let me stop you. I don't see the harm in just sitting with you in here for a little while.'

He picked up his cup and sucked at the edge of the liquid.

'I don't want to spoil the picture on the top,' he said. 'Look.' He held his cup towards her. The barista had made a design on the top of the coffee.

At that moment Maria, the receptionist from the centre, passed by the window. Heather raised a hand to greet her and was hoping she would come in and sit with her. If someone else was there, Nick might be put off and leave sooner, she thought. But Maria walked on.

'It's nice to get you out of that room,' said Nick. 'You have to play a part in there, I know. Now you can be yourself. Now we can arrange to spend some time together and then you'll understand how good it could be. Are you free this evening?'

'No, Nick, I'm not free this evening, or any evening.'

'How about the weekend?'

'No! Apart from anything else,' said Heather, 'I'm twice your age. Old enough to be your mother.'

'The age gap doesn't bother me.'

'You're being ridiculous,' said Heather.

She drank the last of her coffee, put her phone in her bag, pulled on her coat and flung her scarf around her neck. She squeezed out from her seat.

'Usual time next week?' said Nick.

'I'm not sure I can do next week,' said Heather. 'Someone from the centre will call you.'

'When can you see me then?'

'We'll be in touch about your appointment.'

'Don't forget your lunch,' said Nick. He was smiling a strange smile.

Heather grabbed the panini and serviettes from the plate and made her way to the door.

He has unnerved me, good and proper, she thought once she was back in the office. She felt shaky, with a mixture of fury and anxiety. He'd wanted her to be herself and she had been – she'd called him ridiculous, and he was her client. And she'd mentioned the age gap, which was irrelevant, not the point at all. The cheese in the panini was rubbery now it was cold, and she threw most of it in the bin. She tried to call her supervisor, Val, and got voicemail. Fortunately, she was due to have supervision the following day. She fetched a glass of water from the kitchen and went to the window, looked at the bare branches of the trees and breathed deeply, with long out-breaths, to calm herself.

Later that afternoon, when Heather had seen her last client of the day, the phone rang and it was Vicki, the centre manager. She wanted to see Heather in her office.

Vicki was seated behind her large desk. Her brown hair had maroon highlights and was cut in a short style to show off her high cheekbones. She was wearing a black polo-neck jumper adorned with a casually tied floral silk scarf.

'Heather, thank you for coming. Take a seat. Now, tell me,' said Vicki, placing both her hands flat on the desk and leaning towards Heather, 'do you have a problem with boundaries?'

Heather felt colour rising in her cheeks. How could Vicki know about her investigation into Phoebe's death? Who could possibly have told her? Alan? He didn't know she worked at the centre. Not John, please. No, he wouldn't.

'If you do,' continued Vicki, 'we could look at some training, but quite honestly, I'm surprised, a therapist with your experience. You know what I'm talking about, I assume.'

'Well, no,' said Heather.

'You were seen having coffee in Nero with one of your clients earlier today.'

'Oh!' Heather let out a sigh of exasperation. 'That young man waited around after our session and followed me in there. He says he's in love with me. It's erotic transference and I'm going to discuss it in supervision tomorrow. I got away as soon as I could. It was quite unnerving, actually. He's obsessed and very insistent.'

'Goodness, are you all right?' said Vicki. 'Do you need some support around this?'

'I'll discuss it with Val,' said Heather. 'I tried to call her earlier. Maria walked past the café and saw Nick with me. I suppose she told you.'

Vicki and Maria, the receptionist, had become quite friendly of late. Vicki was Maria's line manager and Heather could see that their closeness had mutual benefits.

'Never mind who told me. Is the man a psychopath, do you think? Or on the verge of a psychotic episode?'

'He's damaged,' said Heather, 'more so than I thought at first.'

'Nevertheless, you must look after yourself at all times. Let me know if you need any support, OK?'

As she was leaving the centre, Heather stopped at reception and spoke to Maria.

'Thanks for dropping me in it with Vicki,' she said.

Maria looked up from examining her nails. 'Sorry?'

'You saw me in Nero with that client and you told Vicki. Didn't you see me waving at you? I wanted you to come in and join me. The client followed me in there and I wanted him to leave.'

'Sorry, I just assumed.'

'Well, please don't assume. You could have talked to me first before going to management.'

She'd confronted Maria, in what she hoped was an assertive, rather than an aggressive way, but she couldn't get the business with Nick out of her mind that evening as she cooked and ate dinner, drank coffee, watched some television.

Nick's behaviour had shaken her, and she certainly didn't want to work with him anymore. It remained to be seen how it would play out. Could he see another therapist? Would this incident make her paranoid? Would it affect her work with other clients? Also, when Vicki asked her if she had a problem with boundaries, Heather had thought she was referring to her investigation into Phoebe's death and this had given her a fright. She had certainly overstepped boundaries there. She suddenly wondered what she'd been thinking of, undertaking the investigation. She was putting her job and her whole career at risk. Why was she so obsessed with Phoebe and with finding out how she died? Other clients had died, and it had been sad, but she'd processed it and carried on. Did she really think she'd missed something she should have picked up on and was to blame for her death? Was she projecting something onto Phoebe? She'd told Val that Phoebe reminded her of herself when younger, and that was true. Max had asked her if the whole thing was about Phoebe or herself; he'd asked her that at the very beginning when she'd first talked to him about it in the pub. He hadn't elaborated, but she should have reflected on his question.

Her father had been seriously ill and would need regular support from her from now on. He could have died, yet Phoebe occupied her thoughts more than he did. As she got ready for bed, she thought about her father, in his flat, relying on strangers to help him get up and dressed, struggling to get around and do everyday tasks and probably scared that he might have another stroke, and she felt ashamed and guilty. And then she reminded herself that it was because she'd been there on Christmas Eve and had been able to get him to hospital quickly that he was making such a good recovery; the doctors had said that. It would do no good beating herself up; she would focus on the living from now on and try to think less about Phoebe.

Heather was pleased to see Val the following day. They were in the usual consulting room on the second floor, with mugs of peppermint tea. Val had a tortoiseshell comb in one side of her frizzy brown hair. She smiled at Heather; she had slightly protruding teeth and a lived-in face with creases at the sides of her mouth and by her eyes when she smiled.

'I had a missed call from you yesterday,' said Val. 'I did try to call you back and got no reply.'

'Sorry, I decided it could wait till today, but I should've called again and explained. I was with clients and then with Vicki. She'd asked me to come to her office.'

Val raised her eyebrows. 'Has something happened?'

Heather explained about Nick, the indications of erotic transference in the sessions, him following her to the café and their conversation there. She also related her exchange with Vicki later in the day.

Val frowned as she listened and put one hand up to her mouth, her elbow resting on her other arm. When Heather had finished, Val lowered her hands onto the notepad on her lap.

'He's really overstepped the mark and made you feel

unsafe,' she said. 'You don't need to see him anymore; you know that, don't you?'

'Do you think I should see him once more to explain why I can't work with him anymore?'

'No, I don't. It wouldn't do any good, for him or for you. What he did is alarming and most unusual, and it indicates a degree of disturbance that makes me wonder whether he's suitable for psychotherapy at the moment.'

'You don't think he could be allocated to another therapist?'

'I'm not sure,' said Val. She reached for her tea and took a sip. 'Actually, it's not on that Vicki accused you of having a problem before hearing your side of the story. And she should have reassured you immediately that you don't have to see a client who has behaved in that way.'

Heather was relieved to have Val in her corner, and that she would not be expected to see Nick again.

'What shall I do? I told Nick someone would call him,' she said.

'I'll talk to Vicki,' said Val. 'We have to discuss whether Nick can be offered a service, and someone will contact him. You don't need to do anything.'

'I'd like to know the outcome, whether he is still going to be coming here,' said Heather. 'Will you let me know?'

'Of course,' said Val.

15

Since the start of the year, Heather had been seeing John at least once a week, usually at weekends. They went to restaurants and pubs, had been to Tate Britain together and to a jazz club – Heather hadn't heard of the band or the singers but she enjoyed the atmosphere. She was pleased when John called in the week and asked if she wanted to have lunch the following day. The next day was Friday and Heather was not at the centre; she was at Number 27 and could easily take a long lunch. She agreed to meet John in The White Horse pub at one o'clock.

She had one client booked in on Friday morning. Elizabeth was an interesting young woman, a photographer who was confident in her work but only felt safe behind a camera; her life experience had left her fearful of exposure to people. Heather saw Elizabeth, wrote up some notes and then checked her emails. Mrs Bird was hovering in the passage when she was ready to leave.

'I'm meeting a friend for lunch,' said Heather, 'so I'll be a couple of hours.'

'Male or female?' asked Mrs Bird.

'Male,' said Heather.

'Good,' said Mrs Bird. 'Enjoy yourself.'

Mrs Bird came to the front door and waved her off. It was raining, thin rain like mist that made Heather think of the seaside. She put up her umbrella and waved back at Mrs Bird.

John was there when she arrived. He was sitting behind a table in one of the booths and stood up to greet her. They embraced and he kissed her on the lips. He'd just started drinking a pint of bitter and Heather almost felt intoxicated by the taste of beer on his mouth. She put her umbrella on the floor with her bag, and her damp coat on the back of the chair. She sat opposite John and smiled at him. He smiled back and handed her the large card bearing the menu.

'Pub fare,' he said. 'I hope you can find something.'

'It's fine,' she said. 'I fancy some chips. Cod and chips for me, please.'

John went to the bar to place their orders and returned with a glass of water for her, with a slice of lemon.

'How's your dad?' he asked. 'Did you speak to him on Sunday?'

'He's doing all right,' she said. 'I hope they don't change his carer. He really likes the young woman who comes in every day. I'm going up this weekend.'

'I thought you might be.'

John suggested they take a short break together, somewhere hot; Spain, Italy, Croatia. He could take some time off in May, he said. Heather had a glowing feeling of excitement at the prospect.

'Will you be able to get away?' he asked.

'Of course, I'd love to. It's a great idea. Is that why you wanted to meet today, to plan a holiday? That's really nice.'

The barman brought the meals. Heather squeezed lemon on her fish and shook vinegar and salt over her chips. John had ordered steak and chips. Heather began to eat but he seemed reluctant to start.

'That's not why I suggested lunch today,' he said. 'I've had some news, and I wanted to tell you as soon as I found out.'

Heather felt her stomach lunge. She put down her knife and fork. 'What?'

'A date has been set for the inquest,' he said. 'End of April, the twenty-fifth.'

Heather looked into John's face. His brown eyes were kind, returning her gaze.

'Good, that's good,' she said. 'Let's eat before it gets cold.'

They both began to eat, but after a moment, Heather put down her knife and fork again.

'Will I be called as a witness?' she asked.

'No. You can attend if you want to.'

'You bet I want to,' she said. 'What date did you say?'

She took her diary out of her bag and made a note in the twenty-fifth of April: *PHOEBE INQUEST*.

'What time?'

'Proceedings usually start at nine o'clock. Are you OK?'

Heather realised her shoulders had dropped forward and she'd slumped as if there were a weight bearing down on her back. She sat up straight and pulled back her shoulders.

'Yes,' she said. 'I don't think I really believed they'd

ever set a date. For ages I was waiting for it and then I was sort of drifting along, not thinking about it. And so many other things have happened. I don't know how I feel about it now.'

'Perhaps it will give you some resolution – closure, as they say,' said John.

'Hmm, perhaps,' she said.

Finding out the inquest date was like a trigger, setting off Heather's obsessive thinking about Phoebe again. She'd felt distracted through the rest of her lunch with John and had difficulty focusing in her client sessions that afternoon. After the first client, she told herself she was feeling stupefied because she was not used to eating a full meal at lunchtime. She had a mug of black tea to try and revive herself, but she still had to make a conscious effort not to let her mind drift off as she sat listening to her second client of the afternoon. When he'd left, she packed up and prepared to go home. Mrs Bird tried to detain her with enquiries about her lunch date, but she wouldn't be drawn, just said she had to rush and would see her the following week.

She strode to the underground station, feeling a growing sense of irritation and impatience. She was irritated that she was not going to be called as a witness at the inquest. She wished she wasn't going to Nottingham at the weekend when she had other things she wanted to do and to think about. She wanted to restart her investigation and was thinking it was time to talk to Martin again. She had to know whether he was the young man who went into the off-licence the night Phoebe died.

That evening, she called Max.

'It's good that you're not being called as a witness,' he said. 'It would blow your cover with the family.'

'Christ, yes, so it would,' she said. 'But do I care, if I could help get to the truth about what happened?'

'Of course you care, if you want to continue working as a therapist. They could really make trouble for you if it came out that you've been questioning them and posing as an ex-colleague.'

'Oh, Alan would have a field day, I'm sure,' said Heather.

'If it all goes pear-shaped, you could always become a full-time PI,' said Max. 'There might be a vacancy for you at my old place of work.'

'Maybe I'm not smart enough,' said Heather.

'You're smart enough. You just need to keep the heid.' Just before they said goodnight and ended the call, Max said, 'And keep John onside.'

He'd used the same words when she'd visited him in hospital. Heather thought about that as she looked at Martin's number on her phone. John would not be happy if he knew what she was about to do.

She phoned Martin. He sounded tired and his voice was hoarse. She asked him if he wanted to meet up on Monday, the Easter Bank Holiday.

'Why?' he said and cleared his throat. 'Am I a charity case for you?'

'Not at all,' she said. 'I'm missing Phoebe and I thought you might be missing her too.'

He was quiet for a moment, leaving her hanging; she wondered if he was still on the line.

'There's a fair on the Green,' he said. 'See you there at six o'clock on Monday.'

The line went dead; he was gone. A funfair was not the meeting place Heather would have chosen. For one thing, there would be no chance of recording their conversation on her phone in such a noisy setting. But Martin had agreed to meet her, she had to be satisfied with that.

She travelled to Nottingham on Saturday morning, did some shopping for her father and spent the evening with him. He was frail since the stroke and looked older. He moved about the flat with the help of a stick and could make himself a cup of tea and heat up food in the microwave. He was still having Guinness in the evening, but restricted himself to one can, or so he said. Once a week, one of his friends picked him up in the car and took him to the pub for lunch. He'd been invited to attend a lunch club run by Age Concern and he'd said he would think about it.

'It sounds like the beginning of the end to me,' he said to Heather.

'I don't know,' she said. 'You might enjoy the company.'

'When I'm steadier on my legs I'm going to bowls,' he said. 'That's more my scene.'

She was hoping to see her brother Anthony whilst she was there, but he'd taken his family to Skegness for Easter. He visited their father every weekend when she was in London and ran him around in the car to get whatever he needed – food shopping, books, underwear, Guinness.

On Sunday morning, Heather was relieved to find her father in the kitchen making tea when she came from the guest room. On the way along the corridor she'd had a flashback to Christmas Eve when she'd found him helpless in his chair after the stroke. They had a pleasant morning together. She cooked roast lamb for lunch and then she went for her train. Kissing him goodbye at his front door, she felt a surge of sadness at leaving him and a keen sense of poignancy at their reversed roles, where she was now the carer and he the cared-for dependent.

As the train carried her back to London, the poignant image of her father faded, and feelings of anxiety began to take over. She was apprehensive about meeting Martin and had to admit to herself that there was a large dose of excitement mixed in with the apprehension.

On Monday evening, Heather showered and put on jeans and trainers, T-shirt and a black showerproof jacket and went out to meet Martin. She travelled by bus and arrived opposite Shepherd's Bush Green just before six, crossed the road at the traffic lights and entered the funfair. It was thronged with people, families with children, young couples, groups of giggling girls and boys acting cool. The music was a cacophony, each ride and stall playing a different pop song. She stopped by the dodgems and could make out a fast thumping beat; she thought it might be Meatloaf. It was a perfect accompaniment to the swerving, bumping and jolting inflicted on the occupants of the little cars. She looked around for Martin amongst the brash colours, flashing lights and frantic movement of the rides. At the far side, a bulky red and white contraption swung up above the roundabouts on a massive arm, bearing eight people strapped into seats. Beyond that, chair-o-planes flew in a circle around a central metal structure, gaining height with each revolution.

She walked past spinning teacups, hook the duck, a house of horrors, and found the waltzer. It had been her favourite, and that of her friends, when she was a teenager. They would climb in, the seat swinging from side to side, a strong young man would clamp down the metal safety bar and they would cling to it as the ride picked up speed, spinning the car as it moved round and up and down, and the young man, theirs for a few moments, would give the seat a mighty push and send it into a madder spin and they would scream and laugh. Now she watched as a different group of young girls clung on and shrieked with laughter and another strong young man rode beside them to the sound of "River Deep, Mountain High".

Heather sighed and turned to find Martin next to her.

'Want a go?' he asked.

He looked thinner than when they'd last met, his black hair was straggly, and he had the beginnings of a moustache and beard. He wore a black leather jacket, white T-shirt and jeans. She thought again that he had a seedy, in-need-of-looking-after air about him; she'd thought that when she first met him, at the funeral. There was a smell of alcohol on his breath.

'Hello,' said Heather. 'No, thanks, not just now.'

'I've got these tokens,' he said. He reached in his jacket pocket, took out some coloured plastic discs and displayed them in his cupped hands. His fingernails were not very clean, and one thumbnail was longer than the other. She remembered that he played the guitar.

'Can we just walk a bit first, have a look round?' said Heather.

'Sure.' He put away his tokens.

They walked past a mini roller coaster and stopped to watch the chair-o-planes.

'You don't fancy going on there, I suppose,' said Martin.

Heather laughed. 'You'd have to pay me a vast amount of money to get me on there,' she said. 'When I was younger, yes, I might have gone for it.'

'I'd like to have known you when you were younger,' he said. 'That's not an insult, by the way.'

'If you say so,' she said, and thought, *I was more fun in those days.* She looked into his green eyes; they were glazed; it was difficult to read them. 'How are you, Martin?'

'Oh, fine, I'm just fine.'

He pulled a small bottle of vodka from his inside pocket, took a swig and offered it to her.

'I don't, if you remember,' she said.

'I know, when you were younger, you would have,' he said, and put away the bottle.

They walked on and came to an old-fashioned carousel, its horses still, waiting to set off. The music was the Spice Girls.

'Is this tame enough for you?' said Martin.

'OK, let's go on this,' said Heather.

She stepped up on to the platform and climbed on to a horse on the outside of the carousel. Martin followed and mounted the horse on the inside of Heather's.

The ride started and the horses began to move up and down, and around the carousel, slowly at first and picking up speed, the music loud near the speakers, less loud at the other side. Despite her reservations about doing this with Martin, Heather couldn't help feeling exhilarated by the ride and was again transported back to being a teenager at the fair with her friends. She tried to hear the music from the film *Carousel* in her mind over the raucous music in her ears. *The carousel is romantic; you should be on it with your young man*, she thought, and this brought her back to reality. She looked over at Martin. He was dark, good-looking, with a hint of danger about him, and he could easily have fitted the bill as her boyfriend, years ago. She was relieved to feel the ride slowing down and when it stopped, she climbed off quickly and waited for Martin on the grass.

She could smell onions from a burger van, and there was an ice cream van, but she couldn't see or smell any candyfloss. Martin stopped to look at a shooting range, with cuddly toys as prizes, and she was afraid he might want to have a go and win her a teddy bear. Also, she was wondering when she would have a chance to talk to him.

'Shall I buy you a drink in the pub?' said Heather.

'Let's go on another ride,' said Martin.

'How about this?' said Heather. She pointed to a nearby ride, another she remembered from her youth, with four double seats on the end of each of its arms, seats that lunged forward, first one way and then another and then another, but at least it wasn't high above the ground.

Martin shrugged but reached in his pocket for tokens and went to the kiosk. He stood aside for her to climb into the seat. There was a notice on the inside saying: *Largest person sit this side*. Heather pointed it out to him, and he climbed over her to sit on the inside. As the ride got going, she found herself pressed up against Martin by centrifugal force, as they hurtled this way and that. She was aware of his smell of leather and sweat and alcohol. She closed her eyes and thought about John but was disconcerted by a swooping feeling in her stomach. When they came to a stop, she suggested the pub again.

'I want to sit in a stationary seat, please,' she said.

Martin lit a cigarette and smoked it as they left the fair and crossed the road. They went into a busy pub opposite the green and Heather ordered a pint of cider for Martin and a mineral water for herself. Whilst she was at the bar, she set her phone to record. She joined Martin at one of the small round tables and put her phone on the table. It was noisy, but the phone might pick up.

'Cheers,' he said, and took a long draught of cider.

'How are you really, Martin?' she asked.

'I'm shit. Life's shit and I'm shit; that's what you want to hear, isn't it? It's the truth.'

'You miss Phoebe,' she said.

'You've no idea,' he said, and then he leant forward and fixed her with his green eyes. 'Or maybe you do.'

'I think I do,' she said.

'I know why you're so interested in Phoebe,' he said. 'You were in love with her.' He sat back with a self-satisfied smile on his face.

Heather felt her face grow hot. She did some mental scrambling around to see how she wanted to respond. Her mouth was dry. She picked up her water and took a drink.

'I can see why you might think that,' she said.

Martin raised his eyebrows.

'I wasn't in love with her,' she said. 'I did care about her, though. She reminded me of myself when I was younger. And I'm perturbed by some unanswered questions about what happened to her.'

Martin frowned and began to tap the side of his glass with his fingertips. He suddenly appeared older and more haggard. He looked away, across the bar, and craned his neck to see something or someone. Heather glanced down and checked her phone.

'Someone you know?' she asked.

'I thought it was,' he said. He knocked back the rest of his cider.

'Another?'

'Go on then. I'm skint.'

She picked up her phone and went to the bar. She had to wait to be served. She looked back at Martin. He had his own phone out and looked as if he was checking his messages and sending a message. She paid for his cider and returned to the table.

'Can I ask you something?' she said.

'Here we go. I knew this was a fishing expedition.'

'There's a shop on the corner near Phoebe's flat,' she said, 'an off-licence. Did you go in there on the night Phoebe died?'

'Why are you asking me about the offie, for God's sake?'

'I talked to the shopkeeper, and he said a young man had come in, very upset, just after he'd found Phoebe's body and called the ambulance. I wondered if it was you.'

'No, it wasn't me,' he said. 'No, wait, maybe it was me. So?'

'Martin, you were in the area the night Phoebe died. So? It means you might have seen something.'

'Yes, OK, you got me. I saw her lying there on the ground like a broken doll.' His voice grew louder. 'I see that in my dreams, my nightmares, over and over. I wake up screaming in the night.' People were looking over at him.

She swallowed hard, closed her eyes for a moment, tried not to think about the image Martin had conjured up, to put it out of her mind. She opened her eyes, looked at Martin again.

'Why didn't you wait with her body, go with her in the ambulance?'

'I should have,' he said. 'I know, I…' Tears came to his eyes, and he hunched up his shoulders.

'It's OK, Martin.' She reached across the table and grasped his hand. He tried to pull his hand away, but she held on.

'I used to walk along her street,' he said. 'It's pathetic, isn't it? I'd sometimes ring her intercom and sometimes,' he gave a laugh, like a sob, 'sometimes she'd let me in.'

'Did she let you in that night?'

Martin snatched his hand from under Heather's and wiped his tears away with his fingers. He sat up and picked up his drink.

'I told you before, I wasn't there.'

'Are you sure about that?'

'Fuck you!'

Martin took his drink and headed for the door. Heather guessed he was going out for a cigarette. She didn't think she could push him any further now, so she stopped recording and put her phone in her bag. She followed him outside and found him sitting on the end of a bench seat by a wooden table, with other smokers, a cigarette between his fingers.

'Sorry I upset you,' she said.

'Yeah.' His eyes were glazed again, no sign of emotion in them.

'Thanks for the fairground rides.'

He didn't respond, just took a gulp of cider. Heather thought it best to leave him alone. She walked away to find a bus stop.

16

Heather looked around for Nick when she went to the centre, in case he was following her. Val had told her he would not be offered a service with another therapist. She was relieved, but she still looked about her when she was approaching and leaving the centre, afraid that he might appear. She scanned the faces in the reception waiting area to check he wasn't there. At lunchtimes, she bought food and took it back to her consulting room. When she looked out at the square from the window of her room, she found that she was looking for Nick.

She remembered the session when Phoebe had told her about Martin following her home from work, how a young woman, a stranger, had stopped her and said someone was following her, ducking behind cars and hedges, and Phoebe had looked, and it was Martin. Now Heather was having a parallel experience, and it made her feel closer to Phoebe, helped her to understand how Phoebe might have felt. She also wondered if Martin was as disturbed as Nick appeared to be.

One Tuesday morning, Maria, the receptionist at the centre, said, 'That young man was here yesterday.'

'Who?' she asked, but she knew.

'The one who fancies you. Nick.'

Heather flinched inwardly at her choice of words.

'What did he want?'

'He wanted to know if you were here, number one, and number two, did you work anywhere else. Well, I told him you weren't in, and I said you do work somewhere else, but I wasn't at liberty to divulge that information.'

'Thanks, Maria. I really don't want him pitching up at my private practice.'

'No worries,' she said. Her smile was sickly. Heather suspected she would have liked to give Nick the address of her practice and make trouble for her.

She ran up the stairs to the relative safety of her consulting room and closed the door. She took off her jacket and hung it on the back of the door, sat in the chair behind her desk and leant back.

'Damn him,' she said, aloud. She had enough to worry about, without some lousy stalker. Would he back off if he knew she was dating a police officer? She smiled at the thought. It was a card she would play if necessary. She sat up and reached in her drawer for the key to the filing cabinet. She had several clients to see and would need their notes.

She believed Maria was telling the truth, and that she hadn't told Nick where she did her private work, but she still looked out for him when she went to Number 27. He could find out some other way. She told herself Mrs Bird would be sure to tell her if anyone came looking for her.

One day, she thought she saw him in Chiswick High Road. He was in the distance, and as he got closer she could see it wasn't Nick, but she'd started to feel shaky and anxious. She ducked into a charity shop and looked through a rack of dresses, unseeing, nervous. *It won't do*, she said to herself, *to be so unnerved by a sad and damaged individual.*

She checked in the records at the centre to see where Nick lived. He didn't live in Chiswick. She would have to try not to be paranoid walking around her home area.

She felt like getting away and wanted to see Max, so she called him and arranged a long weekend in Stirling.

It was five hours on the train, plenty of time for unwinding, thinking, reading – she had brought *Strictly Bipolar* by Darian Leader and a Deborah Levy novel, *Hot Milk*. She felt her everyday worries lifting off her as the *Highland Chieftain* bore her northwards, through York, past Durham, crossing the Tyne for a stop at Newcastle, and then breathtaking views of the wild sea over the clifftops of Northumberland, and a longer stop in Edinburgh before the final leg of the journey.

Max met her at the station. He was waiting just beyond the barrier and her heart leapt with joy at the sight of him; joy mixed with sadness at how old he looked now. She kissed the papery skin of his cheek. He smiled with pleasure, took her suitcase and led the way to the bus station. They took a bus up towards the castle, through narrow streets lined with stone buildings, very like the buildings of Edinburgh. His apartment block was near the castle, just off a quiet square and through an archway. He showed her his apartment and then took her down a long ramp of a corridor, to her room. As at her father's place, there was a guest room and Max had booked it for her.

She put away her clothes and walked back up the slope, running her hand along the handrail.

Max's apartment was smaller than his London flat. His old settee and dining table almost filled the sitting room. She noticed he had new chintzy curtains and assumed his daughter was responsible for those. She also noticed a packet of tobacco and a lighter on the table. The kitchen was at the end of the room, not separate. He stood by the cooker, stirring a curry, talking to her as she sat on the settee, leafing through the local paper.

'It's convenient, aye,' he said, 'but the whole place ends up smelling of curry. The extraction system is pathetic.'

After dinner, Max put on the BBC television news channel; the top story was Brexit and there had been another stabbing of a teenager in West London. He asked her if she wanted to go out, which she didn't. He asked her to choose what they watched on television, but she really didn't care; she was just pleased to have his company. Max told her he'd stopped drinking.

'I've knocked it on the head,' he said. 'Six weeks now.'

'That's brilliant,' she said. 'Do you miss it?'

'I do when I watch the football,' he said, and reached for his tobacco and papers. 'I'm only having the occasional smoke now.'

Heather thought it best to say nothing.

'What about you? Do you miss the booze?' he asked.

'It's been a long time for me,' she said. 'Eleven years now. I don't think about it much, but I sometimes wonder if I'm quite boring these days. I don't do much, you know. I don't have much fun!'

'What's fun about staggering about and making a fool

of yourself,' he said, 'and puking and feeling like death warmed up for days, unless you keep drinking?'

'And then there's the retching in the morning and shaking so much you can hardly get that first drink up to your mouth.'

'Yeah, great fun, all that,' he said.

She groaned in agreement. Max got up to put the kettle on.

'There's nothing boring about you now,' he said. 'If anything, it was tedious in the old days having to fend off blokes you'd insulted in the pub and getting you home when you were pissed.'

Heather cringed. After all this time, she could feel as mortified by her own past behaviour as if it had been last week.

'God, I'm sorry,' she said.

'Nah, don't worry. I was as bad. John doesn't find you boring, does he? How is John?'

'He's well,' she said.

The next day, Max took her to see the castle and to an exhibition of local artists' work. She learnt that Stirling was referred to as the brooch that held together the Lowlands and the Highlands of Scotland. In the evening, they went to the Tolbooth arts centre to hear a local band play Scottish folk music.

On the Sunday, they went by bus to Bridge of Allan and had lunch in a pub. Over lunch, Max asked her how she felt now about Phoebe and the inquest.

'I'm nervous about it,' she said. 'I think I should be giving evidence. I don't know why I haven't been called.'

'Anyone can contact the coroner and suggest witnesses, you know,' he said. 'You can suggest yourself as a witness.'

'Can I, really?' She felt a thrill of excitement in her gut at the possibility.

'Yeah,' he said. 'You may be able to submit a written report, at least, if you want to.'

'I'll think about that,' she said. 'Seriously, I had no idea I could do that.' Heather poured gravy over her Yorkshire pudding. 'I saw Martin again,' she said.

'Oh, aye?' Max regarded her, she thought, a little warily.

'He admitted to being in the off-licence near Phoebe's flat on the night she died. But he still maintains that he wasn't in her flat that night. I recorded the conversation on my phone like you showed me.'

'Uh-huh.' Max raised his glass of water to his lips.

'I might have blown it with him, though. I think I pushed him a bit too much. I didn't tell him about the inquest. Do you think I should? Ah, I could use it as bait to get him to see me again.'

'Getting to be quite the hard-boiled detective, aren't you?' said Max. 'Have I spawned a monster?'

'What?' Heather looked into his eyes to see if he was serious. She saw that he was smiling.

That evening, their last together before she returned to London, Heather told Max about Nick and how she'd been feeling paranoid about running into him.

'Och, he's probably crawled back into the woodwork by now,' he said.

'I expect so,' she said.

Max accompanied her to the station the next morning and waited on the platform with her.

'Now, be sure to phone me if you have problems with either of those young men,' he said.

'You mean…'

'Your suspect and the stalker,' he said. 'Not that I can do much from here, but keep in touch, OK? It wouldn't do any harm to tell John about the stalker, would it, eh?'

The train drew in. She looked for her coach and ran to the door, Max walking behind her with her suitcase. She hugged him, boarded the train, stowed her case in the luggage rack, settled into her seat and waved to him as the train pulled out. He waved back, looking small and alone, but smiling. She wished he didn't live so far away, for both their sakes. She sighed and took out her novel, but she didn't open it. She looked out of the window at the outlying houses of Stirling and then at trees and green fields.

It was good that Max had stopped drinking. Pity he couldn't quit the tobacco. Not yet anyway. She'd carried on smoking for two years after she'd stopped drinking. She remembered her last cigarette. She'd used the *Easy Way to Stop Smoking* book, which took a cognitive approach. She read the book twice, and the second time she quit at the recommended stage, taking a day off work for the occasion. She was anxious as she smoked that last one, and excited at the same time. She broke up her remaining cigarettes and threw them in the dustbin, and she had no cravings. In the end, it was easier than stopping drinking.

How had alcohol got such a hold on her? She recalled

the first time she'd been seduced by the magic of alcohol. She was about fourteen. Her mother, Sonia, had taken up with her stepfather, Phillip, and had moved him into their house. That evening, they'd gone out and Anthony wasn't around. For some reason, she'd opened the drinks cabinet and decided to try some Cointreau, as there was plenty left in the bottle and it wasn't likely to be noticed if some went missing. She poured some of the clear liquid into a small glass, took a sip and a lovely feeling of warmth and well-being filled her, right down to her stomach – there was no room for anxiety as this feeling filled her; her worries and fears were gone.

Back then, it became the norm at parties to drink cider and she found she was more at ease after a few drinks and could talk to anyone, and she also felt more attractive and sexy and got off with young men she fancied. Everyone was drinking cider and beer and some of the girls were drinking spirits. It took her a while to get into gin, vodka and brandy with Babycham, but she persevered. Hangovers were par for the course and easily shaken off in those days.

She went to university in Kent to study English and American Literature and added marijuana to the mix and occasionally speed, and she once took LSD. Towards the end of her second year, she began to feel very anxious and emotional, and it seemed to be the general consensus that she was having a breakdown. The GP said she was manic depressive. The remedy? Time at home with her "happy family". She laughed in the doctor's face when he said that. She spent the summer at home and worked in an accounts office. She felt like a zombie. Back on campus for the third year, she had a brief, idyllic romance with a man who had been pursuing her for some time, but it seemed she fell off her pedestal and he ended it. She started hanging around with a drinking crowd and never looked back. She left university with a second class degree and alcohol dependence.

For the next decade, she favoured white wine and beer, with occasional sprees on spirits. Her sexual relationships tended to be with men who were heavy drinkers and were doomed to unpleasantness of one kind or another. She did shop work, waitressing and various office jobs, including at the private investigation agency where she met Max. She began having therapy and after about three years, wanting to commit to a career, she decided to train as a therapist herself. She struggled to limit her drinking and after a number of crises which interfered with her work and study, she agreed to a residential detox. She left the detox unit at Ealing Hospital on a bright, cold March morning and walked, past an off-licence, to the bus stop to begin her new life.

In those early days of sobriety, she attended the local alcohol service, where she joined an evening support group, and in the afternoons she had acupuncture needles stuck in her ears and drank detox tea with other women. For a while she went to AA meetings and they gave her structure and support, but she didn't like the disease model it was based on and the need for the help of a higher power, however loosely that could be interpreted. She felt she'd been helped by her therapist and the detox regime, not any higher power. She disliked describing herself as an alcoholic because of the association with this model. Once she got back to work and study, she stopped the alcohol-focused support, including AA.

That was how alcohol had taken hold of her. As for the "why", she'd explored this in therapy over the years. She had a controlling mother with very high expectations who was never satisfied with her achievements. If she had A grades in everything but maths, Sonia wanted to know why she only had B plus in maths. Sonia wanted her to go to Oxford or Cambridge, but she hadn't got in. She realised that, for her, when she was young, her mother was totally bad and her father, James, totally good. James drank whisky and quoted poetry and talked about Irish mythology. He was a much better and nicer person than Sonia, and she wanted to be like him, and this meant she wanted to drink like him. She was on his side, he was on hers, and they drank together once she was old enough. Another factor was that she was the firstborn child and felt she had to protect her brother Anthony from their mother, to take the brunt of her frustration, disappointment and fury. And then there was Phillip, the usurper of her father's place in the family. Phillip was always on her mother's side, to a slavish extent, and he'd made a number of inappropriate remarks to Heather as she was growing up, like saying she should wear a short skirt to show off her "shapely" legs. These remarks and the way he looked at her made her wary of and uncomfortable with him.

The train was slowing down, and Heather saw that they were drawing into Edinburgh Waverley Station. She was brought into the present for a while by the activity on the platforms and people getting off the train and others getting on and looking for their seats and somewhere to put their luggage. And then they were moving again, and Edinburgh slid past and gave way to open fields.

She wondered if there might be some hereditary element involved in her drinking, some inherited vulnerability. It was difficult to know; it was a disputed area. She did feel that another piece of the puzzle of *why* she'd developed an alcohol problem was that she had received no help or support when she had the breakdown and was given the somewhat careless diagnosis of manic depression by the GP. Indeed, he had been judgemental, attributing her distress to drug taking and he'd said he wouldn't give her any tablets because she would probably take them back to university and sell them. Looking back, she was glad not to have been labelled bipolar and set off on a lifetime of lithium and other drugs. Some therapy at that early stage would have been good, though.

The ticket inspector was making his way down the carriage. Heather smiled at him as she showed him her ticket and he smiled back. She asked him where the buffet car was situated. When he had moved on, she fetched a coffee and a sandwich from the buffet and opened her novel. The young woman in the story had problems with a controlling mother too.

As she came nearer to London, she started thinking about John and looked forward to seeing him again at the weekend. Why hadn't she told him about Nick? It was work stuff and she didn't tend to talk to him about work. But also, she'd felt like a paranoid wreck at times recently and she didn't want John to see her that way; she wanted him to see her as strong. That was how she wanted to see herself; she didn't want to feel at risk of drinking, and mostly she didn't these days, even after Phoebe's death and her father and Max being ill, but the business with Nick had unnerved her.

Just when Heather had stopped thinking about Nick and expecting him to pop up everywhere, she met him in Hammersmith. She came out of Primark and nearly walked into him. He had that strange smile on his face again.

'Hi, Heather,' he said. 'I didn't think you'd go for Primani.'

'What's that?'

He indicated her brown paper carrier bag. 'Primani, that's what the fashionistas call it,' he said. 'I thought you'd be more for the environment, not buying disposable fashion.'

Ridiculously, Heather felt like apologising to him and telling him it was just a pair of pyjamas in the bag. She stopped herself and snapped into therapist mode.

'How are you?' she asked him.

'Not good,' he said, no longer smiling. 'Not since you got me thrown out of therapy. And I haven't found another therapist yet. Not that I think I could trust anyone else after you let me down. In fact, I'm thinking of making a complaint. I can do that, can't I?'

'Or course,' she said, trying not to grimace. 'You can contact the centre and make a complaint if you wish.'

'Would it make trouble for you? I suppose it would, wouldn't it?'

She wanted to say it would be a nuisance, that's all, like a fly buzzing around the room.

'It's your right to make a complaint. We have a complaints procedure.'

'I don't really want to make trouble for you,' he said. 'Look, you're not my therapist now. Can I buy you a coffee?'

'No, thanks, I need to get on,' she said. 'Goodbye.'

She moved to the edge of the pavement, saw a space in the traffic and crossed the road towards the bus stop. She'd been paranoid about seeing him, but in reality, although he was creepy, he was mainly just very irritating.

He called after her, 'Have a nice life.'

17

Saturday morning. Heather smiled to herself, remembering the night before, and at the same time, she felt a familiar knot of anxiety in her stomach. She turned and there was John in the bed, his broad back to her, his dark hair ruffled, his neck somehow vulnerable. She touched his neck and then placed her hand on his back, feeling his warmth, and he roused and turned over to face her.

He smiled and pulled her close to him, murmured in her ear, 'Good morning,' and kissed her neck and then her mouth.

'You won't have to go to work today, will you?' she asked.

'Nope.'

'Good,' she said.

She slid her hand down between his body and hers. He turned onto his back and reached for a condom from the bedside table.

'I wouldn't mind if you had a baby,' he said, as he put it on, 'but you might mind.'

'Hmm, yes, I might,' she said, holding up the duvet to watch, thinking, *did he really just say that?*

The night before, they'd met quite late because John had been held up at work. They'd had supper in a French restaurant and gone straight back to her house afterwards. In bed, she'd clung to him, so relieved to have him with her, and she'd found herself crying. It was not how she'd intended to be.

Afterwards, they sat up in bed and she told him about Nick, how paranoid she'd been about seeing him and how mundanely annoying he'd been when they did meet.

'You probably think I'm making a fuss about nothing,' she said. 'The stuff you have to deal with. Nasty, brutal people, I expect.'

'No,' he said. 'It's not all brutal psychopaths. Very ordinary people can do some of the worst things. You should've told me about it before.'

'Maybe. Nick wouldn't accept the boundaries of the relationship. He crossed a line when he followed me into that café. There's a touch of the psychopath about him, I think.'

'Tell me if he bothers you again.' He reached for her hand. 'Don't worry, I wouldn't get too heavy. I'd keep it proportionate.'

She smiled at him. 'What does that mean?'

'I'd just warn him off,' he said. 'I could always call for back up if necessary.'

'You're joking?'

'Yes.'

She cleared away her papers and files to make enough space on the dining table so they could sit there and have breakfast. John made scrambled eggs, and she made toast and tea. He amused her with tales about his colleagues' charity fundraising schemes. They talked about how they would spend their day together and decided to go to Portobello Road Market. When they'd both finished their eggs, Heather reached for his empty plate. There was something else she needed to tell him; she wanted to get it out of the way and to see how he would react.

'I'm wondering why I haven't been called as a witness at Phoebe's inquest,' she said, placing his plate on top of her own.

John looked straight at her now. 'I wouldn't have thought you'd want to give evidence,' he said. 'What about client confidentiality?'

'Do you recommend witnesses to the coroner?'

'We can do, yes.'

Heather pushed the plates to one side and took a sip of her tea. She felt him watching her.

'I'm thinking of contacting the coroner and suggesting myself as a witness,' she said.

'Why would you do that?' His voice had a cold edge to it.

'Because there may be no-one else who is sure that she didn't kill herself and it was no accident.'

He sat back in his chair. 'Have you remembered something, or found new evidence?'

'Nothing specific. I've been going through my notes, going over and over them actually. I thought at the start that it wasn't suicide, and I haven't found anything to change my mind.'

'Well, I wish you'd drop it, but I suppose that's not going to happen, is it?'

He pushed back his chair, picked up his phone and went to the window. He looked back at her, frowning, thoughtful, and then checked his phone for messages.

They walked around Portobello Road Market and looked at clothes, jewellery, antiques. They ate jerk chicken and rice from a street stall for lunch. John was quieter than usual, she thought. He still touched her, his hand on her back as they negotiated crowds, his arm around her waist when they stopped to listen to a busker, but she wondered if he was angry with her. She looked sidelong at him and was unable to read his face. She bought pears and grapes, green beans, cauliflower, sweet potatoes. He took the carrier bags from her and then he got a call. Of course, it was from work. There had been a serious incident, and his presence was required. She took the bags back from him; he said sorry and kissed her and was off, through the crowd, and she was left standing and wondering about the state of their relationship. Had she damaged it? Would it survive if she went ahead and contacted the coroner? He obviously didn't want her to. Why? Would it undermine his authority? Would it call into question his decision not to investigate Phoebe's death?

She didn't want John to be angry with her. The thought of it made her feel very uncomfortable, and this was not just because it could mean that their relationship was under threat. In the past, when she was drinking, she'd had volatile relationships where the man being angry with her had spelt danger. One in particular, Jim, was ex-army with a short fuse; he was possessive and became jealous if she even talked to another man. On one occasion, he'd thrown a plate at her, with dinner on it, and it had struck her on the temple. There was a lot of blood, but she staunched it, put her white T-shirt to soak in cold water and didn't go to Accident and Emergency. He grovelled afterwards and she forgave him. On another occasion, Jim had punched her in the mouth after she'd had a laugh with some man at the bar when she was getting the drinks in. He'd split her lip, and she should have had a stitch put in it because she was left with a permanent scar on her lower lip; hardly noticeable to others, but a reminder to her.

She knew it was different with John and the alcohol factor was not there anymore, but all the same, she felt anxious at the thought that he might be angry with her. Part of her wanted to placate him, but at the same time, she felt she had to contact the coroner.

The woman who answered the phone at the coroner's office gave Heather an email address to write to if she wanted to make a submission for the inquest. She said the office would be in touch to let her know whether the coroner thought her evidence would assist the investigation.

She didn't want to appear in the courtroom as a witness because she'd lied to Phoebe's friends and family about the nature of their relationship, telling them or letting them think she'd worked with Phoebe at the mental health charity. Phoebe's mother, possibly her stepfather and her friends would be there and if she appeared, they would know she'd been Phoebe's therapist and that she had lied. It could get her into all sorts of trouble. She decided to write a statement that the coroner could read and that could be read out in court if the coroner decided this was appropriate. There was always the possibility that the coroner would require her to take the stand and answer questions. That was a risk she would have to take.

It took several drafts to compose the statement. In the end, it read:

My name is Heather Delaney, and I am a psychotherapist. Phoebe Summers started coming to see me in May 2016 because she had been experiencing anxiety and depression for several years. I saw her on a weekly basis until her death in July 2016. She was drinking heavily at the start of treatment and missed a couple of sessions because of this. To my knowledge, she did not use drugs and was not taking any prescribed medication.

We were working through issues arising from the death of her father when she was fourteen and the subsequent remarriage of her mother. She'd had a number of relationships with men who were abusive towards her. At the start, she had a boyfriend who was physically abusive and controlling. She ended this relationship a few weeks before her death.

During the time I was seeing her, Phoebe never expressed an intention to kill herself and at the time of her death, I would say her mood was improved and she felt more in control of her life. She was doing well in the probationary period of a job she liked at a mental health charity. She was gaining confidence and had cut down her drinking. Her ex-boyfriend continued to call and visit her, and she was worried about this. I was concerned that this ex-boyfriend could have a detrimental effect on her mental health and might pose a risk to her personal safety. We were addressing this in our sessions together.

Oh well, she thought, as she sent the statement by email to the coroner's office, *there's no going back now.*

18

The inquest hearing was scheduled for one thirty in the afternoon at West London Coroner's Court. Heather took a bus and then had a long walk through a residential part of Fulham to get to the court. She was pleased to be walking as her stomach was in a tight knot and she didn't want to arrive. But she had to arrive. She went up in the lift to the waiting room and found it full of people, some sitting round the edge and others standing in groups. A middle-aged woman with a pleasant face and a clipboard introduced herself as a volunteer support worker and told Heather that there were two courts in session and proceedings were running late. She pointed out the people waiting for Phoebe's inquest at the far side of the room. Heather recognised Phoebe's mother, Jean, and her stepfather, Alan. Her friend Sarah was there, in a Gothic black outfit, and a couple of other people, including a uniformed police officer. There was no sign of DI John Kelly. Where was he?

Heather didn't feel comfortable about going to greet the family, so she hung back, went to use the toilet, checked her appearance in the mirror, and then returned to the waiting area and sat near the door with her newspaper. She tried to read the paper but had to keep going back over the same sentence again and again.

At two fifteen, the hearing was announced and Phoebe's family and friends filed into the courtroom. Heather followed and sat at the back. The others had taken seats near the front.

Jean turned round and saw her, so Heather raised her hand and smiled. Jean smiled back, a weak, shaky smile, and said something to Alan. He turned and glared at Heather. She raised her eyes and looked beyond him. On the wall above the coroner's bench was a coat of arms bearing the inscription *Dieu et mon droit*. To the right of the bench was a witness box. To the left, at right angles to the bench, there were two rows of seats against the wall, presumably where the jury would sit, if there was one.

John came in then, with DS Yvonne Simmonds and the uniformed officer. John didn't look at Heather. The officers went to the front and sat down. Heather was both relieved John was there and nervous about what was to come.

A woman entered through a door at the far end of the room and sat behind the bench. She was about sixty, with short, wavy, blonde hair, and wore a smart blue jacket and a blouse with a bow tied loosely at the neck. She put on her glasses and looked at the papers in front of her. After a few moments, she looked up at the people seated before her and introduced herself as Mrs Richardson.

Her voice was mellifluous, her enunciation perfect. 'We are here today because a young woman died and we have to establish who died, where, when and how she came to die. I will call witnesses to give evidence and examine them to ensure I understand everything. Once I've finished with each witness, a family representative can question the witness. When I've examined all the witnesses and considered all the evidence, I will reach a conclusion. It is commonly referred to as a verdict, but it is actually a *finding of fact*. A coroner cannot attribute blame or imply criminal or civil liability. The conclusion may be death from natural causes, accidental death or misadventure, suicide, unlawful killing, or I may record an open verdict, which means that there is simply not enough evidence to reach a conclusion.'

Mrs Richardson poured water from a carafe into a glass and took a sip. A clerk was at the front taking notes on a laptop and she paused her typing as she waited for the coroner to continue.

'I will read out the evidence not in dispute.' Mrs Richardson picked up a sheet of paper. 'The young woman who died was Phoebe Eleanor Summers and she was thirty-three years old. She died on Monday the 18th of July 2016, at 10:55pm, in an ambulance on the way to Charing Cross Hospital. Paramedics attended her address after a 999 call from a member of the public and found her on the ground outside the front of Edith Court, the block of flats where she lived on the fourth floor. She had no known medical conditions. She was seeing a psychotherapist at the time of her death, having presented with anxiety and depression.' She looked up at her audience. 'I will read only the conclusion of the autopsy report, as the full report would be distressing for the family.'

She found another sheet of paper, looked through it and turned to another page stapled to it. Heather found that she was holding her breath. She gripped her handbag. The whole court seemed to be holding its breath.

'This young woman, Phoebe, sustained head, thoracic and abdominal injuries, including a ruptured spleen, consistent with falling from a height. She also had historic fractures of the ribs.' She looked up at the family. 'That means old injuries sustained previously.'

Heather wondered whether Martin had caused the broken ribs. She saw Jean look at Alan and then back towards the front.

'She had a high level of alcohol in her bloodstream at the time of her death.' Mrs Richardson cleared her throat. 'Now,' she said, 'I want to clarify some things so I'm going to call the pathologist who performed the autopsy. Dr Radin?'

The pathologist took the stand, waved away the Bible and made an affirmation.

'Dr Radin, in your professional opinion, what do the injuries sustained suggest about what happened? Were they consistent with an accidental fall? An intentional fall?'

'An intentional fall or jump usually results in more injuries to the legs and spine. The injuries sustained here are consistent with an accidental fall and, in particular, the injury pattern is consistent with that often found when the person has consumed a considerable amount of alcohol; that is, injuries to the face, brain, internal organs.'

Mrs Richardson pulled him up short. 'Thank you, Dr Radin.'

Jean had flinched and lowered her head. Alan put his arm around her.

'So,' continued Mrs Richardson, 'are you saying that, on the basis of the injury pattern, this was most likely to be an accidental fall when under the influence of alcohol, rather than an intentional fall?'

'Yes, ma'am,' he said. 'The only other circumstance that this injury pattern would suggest is that the deceased could have been thrown from a height when unconscious.'

Heather caught her breath and heard whisperings from the people in front, saw movement as people turned to each other. She wanted to jump to her feet and ask the pathologist to elaborate.

Mrs Richardson looked at Dr Radin, her eyebrows raised, and then she looked at her paperwork.

'In your opinion, is it likely that these injuries could have been sustained as a result of a fall from a fourth-floor balcony?'

'Yes, ma'am, such a fall could be responsible for these injuries.'

'Just one more thing. The historic rib fractures, can you tell when these were caused?'

'It's not possible to be exact, but I would say they were sustained within the last two years.'

The coroner invited questions from the family representative. He was a lawyer, tall, slim, about forty-five, in a dark suit. He was sitting next to Jean and appeared to be conferring with her now. He stood and faced the pathologist.

'Roger Hansen. I'd like to pick up on one of your last remarks, Dr Radin. You said the other circumstance this pattern of injuries would suggest is being thrown from a height. Could you say more about this, please?'

Heather inwardly shouted, *Yes!*

'Certainly,' the pathologist replied. 'If someone is thrown from a height, for example, from a balcony, when they are unconscious, their injuries may be similar to those sustained in a fall from that height when drunk. The person would have to be unconscious for this to apply.'

'Thank you,' said the lawyer. 'No further questions, ma'am.'

'Thank you, Mr Hansen. We'll have to rely on our police witnesses to shed light on just how pertinent that comparison is in this instance. Let's hear from them now. Thank you, Dr Radin.'

The uniformed officer took the stand next. He was young and his hands were shaking as he opened his pocketbook. He testified that he had been the first member of the emergency services at the scene; the ambulance had arrived a few minutes later. Phoebe had not said anything; she was unconscious. Several people had come out of the flats, but no-one had seen her fall.

'I understand a shopkeeper called the ambulance,' said Mrs Richardson. 'Did he see anything?'

'No, ma'am,' said the officer. 'Not the fall. Just the young woman lying there.'

'And you went in the ambulance, did you?'

'Yes, ma'am, I accompanied the young woman in the ambulance. The paramedics did all they could, but she died en route to the hospital.'

'And did she say anything in the ambulance?'

'No, ma'am.'

The coroner called DI John Kelly to the stand. He was handsome in his black suit, as he had been at the opera. He swore the oath and then Heather thought he saw her sitting at the back. He looked towards the coroner.

'DI Kelly,' she said. 'You were the officer in charge of investigating the death of this young woman, were you not?'

'Yes, ma'am.'

'I'd like you to tell me how you went about the investigation. What lines of enquiry were followed?'

'A forensic examination was carried out at the scene; evidence was collected in the flat, on the balcony and outside the block. We interviewed the shopkeeper who called the emergency services and the neighbours who came out of the flats after the incident. We conducted house-to-house enquires in the area. We examined Miss Summers' computer and mobile phone and contacted family and friends that she was in contact with. We interviewed the psychotherapist she had been seeing, and her GP.'

'What conclusions did you draw from what you found?'

'No-one in the vicinity had seen or heard anything that was useful to us. There were a number of empty wine bottles in the flat and the toxicology report indicated a high level of alcohol in her system. Given this, and the fact that Miss Summers had been suffering from depression and anxiety in the recent past, it seemed possible that she could have jumped from the balcony or that she fell accidentally.'

'There was no note found, I understand. Isn't there usually a note left if someone takes their own life?'

'Yes, ma'am. That is usually the case, and nowadays it is often something in a social media account, but we found nothing of that kind. However, when alcohol is involved, it can be an impulsive act.'

'Did you consider the possibility that someone else was involved in her death?'

'Yes, I did, but there was no evidence that anyone else was in the flat at the time she fell. One glass had been used and it had Miss Summers' fingerprints on it. There was no sign of a disturbance or struggle. There were other people's fingerprints in the flat and on the balcony, some of which were those of an ex-boyfriend, but we could not establish that there were prints left that evening. He had been there on many occasions.'

The coroner cleared her throat again. 'I am mindful of what the pathologist said about how the injuries could have been sustained. Also a report from the psychotherapist, Ms Delaney, in which she says that Miss Summers had not expressed suicidal intentions, her mood was improved, and that she, Ms Delaney, was concerned about an ex-boyfriend who had been,' she looked at a sheet of paper, '*physically abusive and controlling* and was still calling round and, in Ms Delaney's words, *might have a detrimental effect on her mental health and might pose a risk to her personal safety*. Did you eliminate this ex-boyfriend from your enquires?'

John appeared to take a deep breath, and he placed his hands on the front of the witness box.

'Yes, ma'am. I interviewed the ex-boyfriend on more than one occasion. His DNA was well-represented in the profile we obtained from the flat, but as I said, he had been there on many occasions. He admitted he had found it difficult to accept that the relationship was over, and that he often went to the block where Miss Summers lived in the hope of seeing her. However, he was able to provide an alibi for the evening in question.'

Heather remembered John telling her this. Who the hell had given him an alibi? She knew that Martin was near Phoebe's flat that evening – he'd been in Wahid's shop.

'Did you follow up anyone else whose DNA was found in the flat?'

'Yes, I interviewed Mr Alan Ramsey, the stepfather of the deceased. He had visited her when in London on business. Also, her mother and several other individuals, friends and acquaintances. All were eliminated from our enquiries.'

The family's lawyer was invited to question the witness. John turned to face Roger Hansen.

'These historic fractures of the ribs, DI Kelly,' said Hansen. 'Were you aware of these when you passed the case over to the coroner?'

'I saw the autopsy report, so yes, I was aware of them.'

'As far as the family knows, Miss Summers had not had any accident that could account for these fractures. So you were aware that she may have been subjected to violence in the past – the recent past, we have just heard – but you closed the investigation. Did this possible evidence of physical abuse not ring alarm bells for you? It certainly does for me and for her family.'

'Yes, it did influence the course of the investigation. However, we eliminated the ex-boyfriend and in the absence of any other suspects or evidence of a crime, it was reasonable to conclude that no crime had been committed.'

'This isn't an adversarial court, Mr Hansen,' said Mrs Richardson. 'But your point is taken. Do you have any more questions for the detective inspector?'

'No, ma'am. For the record, I'd like to recommend an open verdict and that the case is reopened by the police as a criminal investigation.'

Mrs Richardson nodded and made some notes. She thanked John, and he and Hansen sat down.

Heather was once again holding her breath. The gangly besuited lawyer had asked some of the questions she would have liked to ask. John would not be so happy with Hansen's interventions.

Mrs Richardson rearranged her papers on the bench and looked at her audience.

'Now,' she said. 'I'm going to sum up. This is very sad for you, the family and friends of Miss Summers, whatever my conclusion. No-one wants to think that their loved one has taken their own life, or indeed that they have accidentally fallen to their death when under the influence of alcohol. In a way, it may be preferable to think that someone else was responsible, however horrific this might be. We can conclude from what the pathologist told us that the injuries from which Phoebe died were caused by a fall from the balcony of her flat. I am persuaded that she did not jump intentionally, because of the pattern of her injuries, the lack of a note or message of any kind and the evidence of her psychotherapist. That leaves us with two possibilities: that it was an accidental fall or that it could have been an unlawful killing.' She sipped from her glass of water. 'DI Kelly has told us that a thorough police investigation was carried out and there was no evidence that anyone else was involved. There was one suspect, and he was eliminated from police enquiries. On the basis of the evidence available, I see no reason to order the police to reopen the case. I conclude that this was an accidental death and that will go on the record today. We may never know how or why Phoebe fell and I understand how heartbreaking that is. I am very sorry for your loss, Mrs Ramsey, Mr Ramsey.'

Mrs Richardson picked up her papers and left the courtroom.

Heather was stunned. She would have liked to sit for a while, but she didn't wish to speak to the family, or to John at that moment, so she slid out of her seat and headed for the lift. As she was going down to the ground floor, she was thinking that the one person she would have liked to talk to was Sarah, Phoebe's friend. She felt that Sarah would share her impatience and disappointment, indeed her anger, at the coroner's conclusion. Did she have Sarah's number? She thought not. How would Jean be feeling now? Jean was probably relieved that suicide had been ruled out, but surely she would have liked the case reopened? She stepped out of the lift and walked out into the street. It was sunny and birds were singing. She'd forgotten it was spring. She wondered if she could wait around and catch Sarah, but she didn't want to get involved with the others, so she strode away from the court, walking briskly to get away as fast as possible. Mr Ramsey, Alan Ramsey – was Phoebe's death a loss for him?

She found herself outside a church. Here was somewhere she could sit for a while in peace, so she went inside and sat in a pew at the back. It was cool and dark, the only light coming in though small windows high up along the nave and a red, green, blue and yellow stained glass window above the altar. She was alone with statues of Mary and the saints, vases of lilies and roses and the Stations of the Cross. She closed her eyes. She felt more than impatience and disappointment, more than anger – she was devastated. She had waited all this time, hoping the inquest would bring justice for Phoebe. The coroner could have delivered it, or at least set the ball rolling; she had not. The coroner had let the police off the hook, probably mindful that they were overworked, and this, in turn, let Martin off the hook. Alibi? What alibi?

The last time she'd been in a church was for Phoebe's funeral. She hadn't cried then, but now she felt her shoulders slump and she cried, more from anger and frustration than distress.

After a few minutes she was sniffing and searching in her bag for a tissue when she heard someone come into the church. And then John was beside her in the pew; he just sat there, not touching her.

'How did you know I was here?' she whispered.

'I'm a detective,' he whispered back.

She couldn't help smiling.

'Are you OK?' he said.

She'd been afraid that he was angry with her and now she was afraid that she was angry with him.

'I didn't know you believed in God,' she said, turning to look at him.

He shrugged.

'You swore the oath,' she said. 'If you don't believe, you should affirm.'

He looked away, towards the altar. 'I'm a lapsed Catholic,' he said. 'It never really leaves you.'

'So am I, but I would've affirmed.'

'Yet here you are.'

She glared at him. 'I just came in here because I wanted some peace.'

'Are you OK?' he said again.

She wiped her nose with a tissue she found in her pocket. 'I'm really pissed off with the coroner's conclusion.'

'And with me?' he said.

'Yes.'

'What can I do?'

'Nothing. Sorry. I want to ask you stuff, but not now.'

'I'll go.' He put his hand on her shoulder for a moment, leaving a tingling heat where he had touched her. 'I'll call you.'

When he'd gone, she rubbed her shoulder. She thought, *I want him to tell me who gave Martin an alibi. But perhaps he wouldn't be allowed to share that information. I'll find out somehow. I'll find out from Martin. Yes, Mrs Richardson, it is heartbreaking not to know what happened. Poor Jean. I must find out for her as well as for myself.*

Right now she wanted a coffee and something sweet to eat. She left the church and went to find a café.

19

On Sunday morning, Heather was surprised to see a car draw up outside her house. It was a brown Audi. Who did she know with one of those? Perhaps the occupants were visiting one of the neighbours. And then a woman opened the passenger door, and it was Jean, Phoebe's mother. The driver got out of the car and slammed the door shut. Alan Ramsey. Heather felt her stomach muscles contract. *My God*, she thought, and then, *thank goodness John isn't here.* She considered ducking down and pretending she wasn't in, but no, there was nothing for it but to invite them in and face whatever music they had in store for her. She went to the front door and opened it.

Alan Ramsey stood there, as he had on that previous occasion, but without his briefcase and clipboard. Again, she was struck by his muscular build, sun-tanned face and blue eyes. This time she would not have described his face as pleasant, because she remembered his hostility at the end of their meeting and in the courtroom, though today he looked beleaguered rather than hostile. He wore the navy bomber jacket he had worn last time he was there, with black trousers and an open-necked white shirt. Jean stood slightly behind him. She wore a knee-length denim skirt and denim tunic top, and she held a black handbag in front of her, like a shield.

'One day a few months ago, you called in on me,' Jean said. 'I hope you don't mind me calling on you.'

'No, of course, come in.'

'Alan knew where you lived,' said Jean, as Heather showed them into the sitting room.

Heather moved a clothes horse of damp washing from the middle of the room to the far end by the French window. She cleared her newspapers from the coffee table.

'Please sit down. Can I get you some coffee?'

They both said yes to coffee, so Heather escaped to the kitchen and put the kettle on. So, Jean and Alan were not just back in touch with each another – he had stepped up to the plate for her now. What did they want? Had they realised she was the psychotherapist referred to by the coroner? Had she avoided exposure in the court, only to be outed now by these two? She gripped the edge of the sink and stared, unseeing, out of the window.

She returned to the sitting room to ask how they wanted their coffee. They were sitting side by side on the settee and answered her questions about milk and sugar. She was aware of putting off the moment when they must talk.

She brought in the coffees and sat in a chair at right angles to them. 'What can I do for you?' she asked.

Again it was Jean who spoke. 'When you came to see me, you asked me a lot of questions about Phoebe. You said you didn't think she killed herself. Then you had Alan round here, asking him questions.' They looked at each other, briefly. 'And then you were at the inquest.'

'Are you the psychotherapist?' said Alan.

'Yes,' said Heather.

'You said you worked with her,' said Alan.

Heather wanted to say, *I did work with her*, but instead she said, 'I'm sorry. I misled you about that.'

'That's not all you misled me about, pretending you wanted work doing. And I felt you ruddy well suspected me of something.'

'It doesn't matter about any of that now, Alan,' said Jean. 'The thing is,' she addressed Heather, 'you wanted to know what happened to Phoebe and no-one else seemed to care. And now, that inquest verdict, conclusion, or whatever you call it. I couldn't believe it.'

'I know,' said Heather. 'I wanted the coroner to record an open verdict and direct the police to reopen the case.'

'Yes,' said Jean. 'That's what our solicitor expected to happen.'

'Is there an appeal process?' asked Heather.

'No, there isn't. It is possible to challenge a coroner's decision, say, if the inquest wasn't carried out rigorously, or there's new evidence, but we have no grounds to challenge it.'

Heather nodded. The ticking of the clock on the mantelpiece seemed loud; she didn't usually notice it.

'We wondered,' said Jean, 'whether you, as Phoebe's therapist, might have some insight into why this happened to her, something everyone else has missed.'

If only, thought Heather. *I should have, but I've failed her.*

Jean was leaning forward, her head on one side, her eyes on Heather, an earnest expression on her face. She was no longer the stoical parent she'd presented at the funeral and when Heather had visited her. She was now desperate to know what had happened to her daughter. Alan was looking at Jean.

'I wish I had,' said Heather. 'Believe me, I've been over and over the notes I made when I was seeing Phoebe. I can't find anything that would explain what happened.'

'Nothing?' said Jean, her voice louder. 'Really? How long was my daughter in treatment with you?' Her eyes were blazing now. At last, Jean was the fiery, angry mother Heather had expected her to be.

'I'd been seeing her for ten weeks.'

'Oh, that's not long, I suppose. Anxiety and depression, the coroner said.' Jean looked as if she wanted to say more and then changed her mind.

'I did say in my statement to the coroner that she'd never expressed an intention to kill herself.'

'Thank you for that, anyway,' said Jean.

'The boyfriend,' said Alan, 'do you know where he is? I'd like to have a word with him.'

'I'm sorry, no, I don't.'

It felt strange that she was protecting Martin from Alan, but she saw no point in letting Alan loose on him. It would do no good and could possibly do harm, in particular to Martin.

'Did you ever meet Martin?' she asked him.

'No, why?'

'When you were here before and I mentioned Martin, you said he was a toerag, so I wondered if you'd met him.'

Jean was looking at Alan now, awaiting his reply.

'No, I never met him, but I heard enough from Phoebe to know what an excuse for a man he is.' He turned to Jean. 'She told me about him when I was up in London and went to see her. Sorry I didn't tell you at the time.'

Jean reached across and took Alan's hand. Heather remembered Phoebe telling her about Alan coming to see her. And then she thought about Sarah.

'Look,' she said. 'I want to carry on asking questions and trying to find out what happened. Is that all right with you?'

Jean nodded. 'Yes, you're probably better placed to do it than I am.'

'You may be able to help,' said Heather. 'For instance, do you have a phone number for Phoebe's friend Sarah? I might want to talk to her, and I don't have her contact details.'

'Yes, I have her number.' Jean took her mobile out of her handbag and scrolled down her contacts. 'Here you are. Sarah Smart.' She handed her phone to Heather and Heather fetched her own phone from the dining table and entered the number.

'Are you supposed to be doing this, discussing a patient, asking people questions?' said Alan. 'Aren't there professional boundaries when you're a therapist?'

'That's right,' said Heather. 'I can only continue if I can rely on you two to keep it between us.' *And I don't tell my lover, Detective Inspector John Kelly*, she thought. *If only I were involved with someone else, but you can't choose who you fall in love with, can you?*

'We won't tell anyone,' said Jean, giving Alan a

warning look. 'Do what you need to do. Just find out what happened to my little girl.'

When they'd gone, Heather flopped in the chair for a few minutes, her arms loose at her sides. *Well, that could be good, or it could be very, very bad*, she thought. And then she got up and looked for her Phoebe notes. She found the session she wanted, towards the end of their time together:

Phoebe cheerful. Probationary period at work going well.

'I'd like to see my mum.'

P silent for a few minutes, then said her mum must have been devastated when Dad died. 'She adored him. None of this is her fault, I can see that now.'

Mum had "turned herself off" when he died and didn't seem to care about P at all. Then she met Alan and, 'There was a spark again. He brought her alive for a while.' So P felt she should not blame her for marrying Alan.

I suggested P might have felt Mum should turn to her, rather than to a new husband. P agreed.

Perhaps P felt shut out? P said yes. 'But we might have got closer as time went on.'

NB P able to put herself in her mother's place and imagine things changing for the better.

She said she had cut her mother out of her life and had seen Alan more than Mum recently.

I prompted, 'And now you'd like to see her.'

P said yes; she missed her.

> *I said she could go and see her mum.*
> *P asked if Mum would want to see her now and*
> *I said, 'I'm sure she would.'*

The session was not long before Phoebe died. She never got to see her mum. Heather thought she should tell Jean that Phoebe had wanted to see her. It might be of some comfort to her.

Heather had told John that she was probably going to Nottingham that weekend to see her father. In fact, she hadn't intended to go away; she wanted some time to herself. And then Jean and Alan had turned up. She could hardly believe it.

That evening, she decided to catch up with her father and Max. She rang her father first. He took a while to get to the phone but sounded all right once he was on the line. She could tell he was delighted to hear from her. He told her he'd started going to the Age Concern lunch club two days a week.

'They do a good shepherd's pie,' he said. 'And apple crumble and custard.'

'Good hearty food then, Dad. They'll fatten you up nicely.'

'Oh, I don't put weight on, you know me; I can eat anything. And they've a pool table and darts there.'

'That's great,' said Heather. 'Have you made any new friends?'

'Some of the lads play a passable game of darts,' he said. 'And there's a woman called Betty who is, shall I say, keen on me, but I'm not sure I should encourage her.'

'Oh, why not, Dad? Is she attractive?'

'Not bad for an old 'un, not bad at all. She's got a twinkle in her eye.'

Heather came off the phone feeling reassured that her father was doing fine and was actually enjoying a social life. Now for Max. She was a bit apprehensive about calling him, worried that he might be drinking again. But she had a lot to tell him, so she keyed in his number.

'Hello, stranger,' he said. 'I was wondering if we'd fallen out, it's so long since you've called.'

'You can call me, you know, Max.'

He said these days she was the busy one and he was idle, so he thought it best to wait for her to call.

'What's new, hen?'

She told him about the inquest and the coroner's conclusion and how she was stunned at first and then angry. He listened, just saying "uh-huh" now and again.

'Well, say something,' she said.

'I'm not surprised,' he said.

'Oh, well you might be surprised when I tell you who came to see me today.'

She told him about Jean and Alan and how they now knew she was Phoebe's therapist and Jean wanted her to find out what happened.

'Alan was a bit hostile, and Jean was angry that I hadn't got any answers for her, so it was difficult. But I got a phone number for Phoebe's friend, Sarah, and I'm going to try and set up a meeting with her.'

'What do you hope to get from that?'

'I'm not sure,' said Heather. 'I just know that after the inquest I wished I could talk to her.'

'Do you trust Alan not to report you for professional misconduct?' asked Max.

'I don't know, but what choice have I got?' she said. 'I'm hoping he wants to stay in Jean's good books and that will be enough to keep him in line. Now, what about you? Are you still sober?'

'As a judge. And you're right, it's boring as hell.'

'Oh, don't say that!'

'Nah, don't worry, I'll stick with it.'

20

The Sly Fox poetry and music evenings took place in the back room of a pub. Heather bought a ginger ale and went through to the back. There was no-one on the door; it was free to go in. The room was dimly lit except for the small stage, at the far end, which had green curtains at the back and a microphone stand at the front. Pub tables and chairs were arranged around the stage as for a cabaret and most were occupied, mainly by people in their twenties and thirties, with a few older. Many people were talking animatedly, others were waiting quietly, some looking at notebooks or sheets of paper. Heather scoured the room, saw Sarah and made her way over, squeezing between chairs. Sarah was dressed in black, as usual, and her eyes were black with kohl. She pulled out a chair for Heather.

'Hi,' said Sarah, raising her voice above the hubbub. 'You found it then.' She leant towards Heather. 'The inquest result was shit. That was no accident, trust me. My mate is on first. We'll have time to talk later.'

Heather nodded and they both turned towards the stage. A man of about fifty in a pork-pie hat and spiv jacket was climbing the steps onto the stage. He tapped the microphone, and a hush fell over the room.

'Thanks, folks.' He took a small piece of paper from his inside pocket and proceeded to tell jokes, mostly one-liners about items in the news, with a left-wing slant. The audience loved him and laughed uproariously. After five minutes or so, he stopped and raised his hand and said what a great line-up they had that evening and introduced the first act, a young man with a guitar who was waiting at the side. The compere jumped off the stage and the young man sang two songs, one about social media and the other about the pitfalls of dating. When he'd finished, the young man came to Sarah's table. He and Sarah kissed each other's cheeks, and he sat down next to her. Heather smiled at him, and he smiled back.

Next up was a young blonde woman with a sad poem about lost love and a more upbeat one about her cat. She was followed by a young black man with a moving poem about a friend who'd died. An older woman with a mane of frizzy red hair got up next and delivered a rant about the need for a revolution to get rid of inequality and redistribute wealth. Heather was impressed by the enthusiasm and eloquence of the performers and thought it was good that so far they had all known when to stop and not gone on for too long.

And then the lights went up and it was the break. People started getting up to go to the bar and the toilets. Heather turned to Sarah.

'I'm enjoying it,' she said. 'I didn't realise what I was missing.'

'Yeah, it's cool,' said Sarah.

Sarah introduced her to Jake, the young man with the guitar, and to the other people at the table, saying, 'Heather knew Phoebe.'

Several of them murmured expressions of empathy:

'I'm so sorry.'

'It was terrible.'

'We all miss her.'

Heather smiled and nodded and turned back to Sarah.

'I saw you at the inquest,' said Sarah, 'and then you pissed off.'

'Yes,' she said. 'I would've liked to talk to you, but I had to leave.'

Sarah had a questioning look. 'Jean was really upset,' she said.

'I thought the verdict was rubbish, too,' said Heather. 'It's not possible to challenge it unless there's new evidence.'

'God! Like what?'

'I don't know at the moment. Does Martin come here?'

'Not anymore,' Sarah replied. 'I don't think he'd dare show his face here now.'

'When we talked after the funeral, you said Phoebe had met someone new. Can you tell me about him?'

Sarah's face lit up. 'I can do better than that,' she said. 'I can introduce you to him. Come on.'

She stood up and reached for Heather's hand. Heather grabbed her handbag from the floor and allowed Sarah to lead her between the chairs and tables and out into the pub. Sarah peered at the people clustered around the bar, grinned at Heather, led her forward and tapped the shoulder of one of the young men. He turned and smiled at her and said, 'Hi, how're you doing?'

He was tall and rangy, with red hair curling on his neck, blue eyes and a pleasant face. Sarah introduced him; his name was Toby. He and Sarah had a conversation about a mutual acquaintance. He seemed a really nice young man, but all Heather could think was that he didn't seem Phoebe's type at all. Phoebe had talked about a number of past boyfriends and Heather thought of Martin as her type: dark, good-looking, needy and dangerous. Toby was too nice, too fresh-faced and jolly. He was laughing now, an open, relaxed laugh. And then Sarah was telling him that Heather had worked with Phoebe and wanted to ask him about her, and he grew serious.

'Hi, Toby,' said Heather. 'I'm trying to piece together what happened to Phoebe and talking to anyone who knew her, really. I hope you don't mind.'

'Ah, man, that was so sad about Phoebe,' he said, shaking his head. 'I only met her a couple of times, but I really wanted to get to know her better. She was a beautiful person.'

'Yes, she was,' said Heather. 'Where did you meet her?'

'I met her here,' he said, 'and I asked her if I could see her at the weekend. We met up on the Saturday and had a Thai meal and then some drinks in O'Neill's.'

'Did she seem OK that evening?' asked Heather. 'Did she seem depressed or troubled?'

'Not at all,' said Toby. 'She was good company. She got a bit tipsy, and I thought she enjoyed herself.'

'Forgive me, this is going to sound very intrusive,' said Heather, 'but did you go back to her flat that night?'

Toby raised his eyebrows and backed away slightly. 'Wow,' he said. 'Have you ever thought of being a cop?'

'Sorry to be so blunt,' said Heather, 'but I cared about Phoebe and it's important.'

'No, I didn't,' he said. 'I just saw her into a taxi. She told me things had got heavy with her previous boyfriend and she wanted to take things easy.'

'Thank you so much,' said Heather. 'Did you see Phoebe again?'

'No, sadly, that was the last time I saw her. We texted each other and I spoke to her on the phone on the Sunday. She seemed fine then. We were going to meet up in the week. The next thing I knew, the police told me she was dead. They got my details from her phone. They asked me pretty much what you've asked me. I was really cut up about it.'

Heather thanked him again and he said goodbye to them both and went to the bar.

When they got back to their table, Heather said to Sarah, 'He seems nice, but not at all Phoebe's type.'

'I know what you mean,' said Sarah, 'but he might have been good for her. A bit of normality and fun, instead of being stifled and watched all the time.'

Heather nodded. 'Yes, he might have been.' She took a sip of ginger ale. 'Martin would've been very jealous if he'd known about that date, wouldn't he?'

'He'd have gone ape,' said Sarah. 'Maybe Phoebe didn't invite Toby back in case Martin was hanging around.'

They both looked towards the stage, where the second half was about to get started. A small woman was trying to lower the microphone and the MC in the pork pie hat came to her aid.

'Are you reading tonight?' Heather asked Sarah.

'No, I'm kind of blocked at the moment,' said Sarah. She sighed, and then smiled. 'It'll come back though. It's happened before.'

The woman on the stage read an intense poem, full of images of wind and sea, followed by two more poems. Heather tried to listen, but she was feeling distracted now and couldn't keep her attention on the performance. When the woman had finished and was leaving the stage, to applause and cheering, Heather turned to Sarah and leant in towards her.

'Do you know who gave Martin an alibi for the night Phoebe died?'

'No,' said Sarah. 'I haven't talked to him. Have you?'

'Yes,' said Heather, 'and it looks like I'll have to talk to him again.'

Friday evening and Heather had just come off the phone to John. For the last two weeks, she hadn't wanted to see him; she was too angry with him – for giving up on the investigation into Phoebe's death, for not calling her as a witness at the inquest, for the inquest conclusion, though that was hardly his fault. So she had put him off, and now she wanted him with a physical hunger that took her by surprise. She wanted to see his face, to talk to him, to feel his touch, to sleep beside him. But he was on an important case and couldn't see her until Sunday. She had to get through Friday night and the whole of Saturday. He was apologetic, but she wondered if he was doing it on purpose, to punish her for pushing him away. She wished she'd arranged to go to Nottingham to see her dad or arranged to see a friend that evening. Who was around and might be free? In the old days, when she was drinking and trying to cut down, Friday night was difficult. She'd feel like letting rip to celebrate the end of the working week. If she could get through Friday night without drinking, the rest of the weekend would be easier. The Friday tension and restlessness had simmered, until she took that first sip of wine. She felt a bit like that now and it was unnerving.

And then she saw the brown Audi draw up outside. This time it was just Alan Ramsey who got out; Jean was not with him. What the hell did he want? She had a bad feeling about it and felt her heart thumping. She took a deep breath and breathed out slowly. The bell rang and she went to open the front door.

Alan looked like he'd come straight from a building site. His checked shirt, jeans and work boots were dusty with plaster.

'I want a word,' he said.

Heather stood to one side, held the door open for him. He made an attempt to brush down his clothes with his hands and stamped his feet a couple of times. He stepped inside. Heather glanced down at his large, dusty boots.

'I could take off the boots,' he said.

'If you would, please.'

He prised them off and stood in green woollen socks. He was an inch shorter without the boots, but still imposingly large and muscular. Heather led the way into the lounge and indicated the settee. She wanted him sitting down, not standing over her. She sat in the armchair.

'Jean trusts you, for some reason,' said Alan, sitting and crossing his legs. He looked tense and uncomfortable.

'And you don't?' she said.

'Well, she's desperate,' he said. 'I'm not, and I wouldn't trust you as far as I could throw you.'

Heather felt hurt and indignant for a moment, and then she reminded herself that she had deceived a number of people recently and Alan Ramsey was one of them. It occurred to her that he probably was desperate about something, or he wouldn't have come to see her.

'Fair enough,' she said. 'But now you know I was Phoebe's therapist, and I hope you can understand that I was in an awkward position.'

'Yeah, sure,' he said. 'How's your *investigation* going?' He mimed quotation marks when he said the word.

'I'll let Jean know if I have anything new. Do you want some tea?'

'Do you have a beer?'

'I don't keep beer,' she said. 'I could make tea.'

'No, forget it. I wanted a word because... well, I wondered what Phoebe said about me in those sessions with you.' He folded his arms across his chest.

Ah, so that was it; that was what he was desperate about. It must have been playing on his mind.

'Is there something in particular you're worried about?' asked Heather.

'Phoebe had a vivid imagination,' he said, 'and she was quite vulnerable, so... I wondered what she said about me, that's all.'

'Hmm, well,' said Heather. 'The sessions were confidential, but I suppose I can tell you a couple of things. Phoebe said you were good for her mum, but she didn't realise it for a while and resented you.'

Alan nodded. 'She did, yes.'

'She said you wanted to come to London and sort out a boyfriend who was abusing her. She appreciated that.'

'Yes, that's right.' He shifted in his seat, rubbed his nose. 'So she didn't tell you there was anything inappropriate in my behaviour towards her?'

Heather paused for a few moments, watching his face and demeanour. He looked tense and nervous, but he didn't look shifty or guilty. He was looking straight at her, awaiting her response.

'Was there anything inappropriate to tell me about?' she said.

'Fucking hell, no,' he said. 'But god knows what went on in her head.'

Heather felt a surge of anger on Phoebe's behalf.

'I've got a question for you,' said Heather. 'Did you visit Phoebe again after that time when you took her for lunch in an Italian restaurant?'

'Why?'

'I wondered if you saw her again nearer the time of her death. In case you can shed some light on her state of mind.'

'No, no, I didn't,' he said. 'I was going to, but I didn't make it because of a job. Could it have made a difference?' He shrugged. 'I don't think so.'

'You're probably right about that,' she said. 'And you never met Martin?'

'I've already told you, no,' he said. 'You haven't answered my question.'

Heather raised her eyebrows.

'Did she say I did anything inappropriate?' he said.

'Ah, that question. Actually, no, she didn't.'

Alan relaxed visibly and sat back with a sigh. Then he moved forward again on the seat and turned his shoulders, his whole body towards her.

'I don't particularly want Jean to know I was here today,' he said. 'Understood?'

'Loud and clear,' she said.

'One more thing,' said Alan. He had regained his confidence; his nervousness had gone, and his eyes were bright blue and piercing. 'I want something else to be clear. I'm going along with this, with you, for Jean's sake. If you put a foot wrong, if you mess things up for Jean or you mess things up for me with Jean, I could make things difficult for you.'

He stood up and seemed to puff out his chest and shoulders. Heather stood up too.

'I've no desire to mess things up for you,' she said. 'I just want to find out what happened to Phoebe.'

'OK, just so you know.'

He walked past her into the hall and put on his boots. Heather opened the front door.

'You'll be in touch then?' he said.

'Yep. With Jean.'

Heather closed the door behind him and leant her shoulder against it, listening to his footsteps on the path and the car starting up and driving away. Shit, what was that? Did that really happen? Again, after an encounter with Alan Ramsey she was left shaken.

21

'Where are we going?'

John had picked Heather up at ten in the morning. It was the first time she'd been driven by him, and she hadn't seen the car before – it was a blue Ford Fiesta and belonged to his ex-wife, Claire. His own Mondeo was in for a service.

'I thought we'd go to Margate for the day.' He turned to her. 'Is that all right with you?'

'I wish you'd told me before. I'd have brought my swimming costume.'

'Really?'

'No.'

Heather looked at his profile. He'd been working long hours on the case, and she imagined he'd been eating junk food and neglecting to shave, but today he was clean shaven and alert. She watched his strong hands on the wheel. He drove confidently, his expression intense, his brown eyes on the road, the mirror, looking left and right, missing nothing. He changed gear and returned her gaze, smiled at her. She'd been waiting for that smile.

'What?' he said.

'Nothing. I've missed you.'

'Good. I've missed you too. They're a great team at work, but there's a constant need to make wisecracks, you know?'

'I'll try not to make too many then.'

He glanced at her. 'I find it restful being with you; you know, calming.'

'Really?'

'Yes. It's smart-aleck lawyers as well,' he said. 'I'm sick of them.'

'So you find it restful being with me because I'm not funny or smart.'

'Fishing for compliments now?' he said. 'Ah, what's this, then?'

He slowed the car down and came to a stop, just short of the bumper of the car in front. It was a sunny day in May and a lot of drivers had taken to the roads. This was just the first of several traffic jams they got stuck in before they were out of London. John reached across her and opened the glove compartment.

'Do you want to put on one of these CDs?' he said. 'They're Claire's, so I don't know what they are.'

Heather selected an Annie Lennox album and put it in the player. The song was "There Must Be an Angel".

'Glorious voice; I'd forgotten. Do you like this?' asked Heather.

'It's OK,' he said. 'Yeah, I like this track.'

'Nice of Claire to lend you her car.'

John let off the handbrake and the car rolled forward a few yards. The traffic began to move, slowly.

'You must be on good terms with her,' said Heather.

'Good enough,' said John. 'I need to be,' he turned to her, 'because of the kids.'

'Of course. Sorry.'

He turned to her again. 'Does it bother you?'

'No.' Heather felt foolish. 'Well, a bit, yes. Children must make a strong bond between you.'

'We could have a child.' His eyes were on the road again.

There. He'd mentioned it again. Rather than feeling reassured and happy, Heather felt irritated and panicky at the thought that she was keeping so much from him. But it was not the time or place to explore her reservations and confusion.

She just said, 'Let's see how it goes.'

A couple of traffic jams later, they hit the A2 and began to move faster. On the M2, the traffic kept flowing and soon they were motoring through proper Kent countryside, with green fields, orchards, and oast houses, past signs to Whitstable and Herne Bay, and into Margate. The wide bay swept round, a perfect yellow sand beach and glittering sea, and the huge sky was almost completely blue, with just a few fluffy clouds.

'Turner admired the sky here more than any other,' said Heather.

They drove slowly along the front, past the whirling and spinning lights and music of the reopened Dreamland funfair. John turned into the back streets and found a parking space. It was twelve o'clock and they agreed that they wanted a coffee before anything else. They walked back down to the front and along the promenade.

There were people on the sands, young couples with small children, older couples in deck chairs, a group of teenagers throwing a frisbee between them. A few people were paddling in the sea, or further out, swimming.

'Want a paddle?' asked John.

'Not particularly,' she said. 'It's not hot enough to get me in the water.'

There were several cafés with outdoor tables, so they picked one and Heather sat at a table while John went inside for the coffees. She checked her phone for messages and found none.

'She's bringing them,' he said, joining Heather at the table. 'Remember I suggested a holiday together? Preferably somewhere hot enough to get you in the water. I'm still up for it, if you are. Thank you,' he said to the young waitress, bestowing a charming smile on her, so that she blushed as she put down the coffees and a jug of milk.

Heather smiled to see the effect he had on another woman, feeling gratified and insecure at the same time. She poured milk into her coffee.

'I'd love to go on holiday with you, John,' she said. 'But are you sure now is a good time?'

'Why?' he said. 'We've nearly got this case wrapped up. But I somehow get the feeling it's not a good time for you. We did say May, I think. But if you want to delay it, just say.'

'If we could. Sorry.' She did an apologetic grimace, which she knew was overdone and false and she felt sure he would pick this up.

'Let me know, then,' he said. He was examining her face, first her mouth and then her eyes.

'It's just I'm quite busy for the next week or two,' she said.

'Fine. Don't worry. Let me know.'

He poured a few drops of milk into his coffee and stirred it slowly.

Heather looked out at the sea and allowed a silence for a moment, hoping the awkwardness would pass. She turned back to John.

'I like the museum here,' she said. 'It's just round the back in the old town. If you haven't been, shall we go?'

'Yes, let's do that,' he said.

When they'd finished their coffee, they walked into the atmospheric streets of the historic old town.

'I love this bit of Margate,' said Heather. 'Here's the museum.'

The museum building had formerly been the police station and magistrate's court. The curator was delighted to have a policeman visiting and gave them a guided tour of the courtroom and police cells and of the nautical history exhibition. By the time they came out, they were both hungry, so they headed for the café at the Turner Contemporary. The gallery stood, like a strange white ship of the future, on a promontory at the end of the beach.

They looked at the lunch menu. Heather chose the healthy vegetable soup and wholegrain roll. John complained the food was all butternut squash and wilted spinach, and then he found a smoked bacon sandwich and went for that. He was more of a carnivore than Heather and she thought he could do with more vegetables in his diet. The café was busy, but they found a table near the window and were able to look out over the beach and the sea as they ate.

John lifted the top of his sandwich and took out the salad leaves, saying, 'Why spoil a bacon sandwich?' He went to look for brown sauce and returned with sachets of HP.

'I sometimes think about moving down here,' said Heather, 'it's away from the pollution and frantic busyness of London, but it's culturally up and coming.'

John raised his eyebrows. 'You wouldn't really like it, would you?' he said. 'The old town's quaint enough and this gallery is fantastic for the town, but otherwise it's still quite run-down. And you do know the council is run by UKIP, don't you? I can't see you liking that very much.'

'I know, but I get fed up with London sometimes. I come from a smaller city, Nottingham. It's more manageable somehow, more on a human scale. Have you always lived in London?'

'Kilburn born and bred,' he said. 'I wouldn't want to leave London. I'd be bored stiff in a small town or a village, couldn't stand it.'

'What about the sea, though? What about this?' She indicated the view. 'Don't you love the sea? It has a restorative effect, you know, calming, good for the soul.'

'I can see that,' he said. 'I love a day out by the sea, or a holiday. But I wouldn't want to live here. Think what it would be like in the winter. Storms, big waves, wind. No thanks!'

'They have a jazz festival here.'

'Still no thanks.'

'It's just a dream of mine that I go to when things feel difficult,' she said.

'Do things feel difficult in your life right now?' said John. He was frowning and looking intently at her. 'Anything you want to tell me about?'

'Oh, you know. Phoebe's death. My dad being ill and Max, and the inquest and that weird stalker bloke I told you about. It all got on top of me for a while, but I'm OK now.' She attempted a bright smile. Part of her wanted to tell John everything – about visiting the off-licence near Phoebe's flat and meeting with Martin, and about Jean and Alan coming round and them knowing she was Phoebe's therapist, and Jean wanting her to find out what happened to Phoebe, about talking to Sarah and meeting Toby, and then Alan coming round again and being vaguely menacing – but she bit her lip and stopped herself. He would be annoyed at her meddling and her implied criticism of his investigation and his professional judgement; it was obvious she didn't think he'd done his job properly. Didn't she want his protection where Alan was concerned? Yes, but if she told him about Alan's visit, it would mean telling him Jean and Alan now knew she was Phoebe's therapist. He was bound to think that was stupid and ill-advised. And it would probably involve telling him she planned to continue to investigate Phoebe's death. Also, she had been keeping some of these things from him for so long, how could she tell him now?

'I'm sorry I pushed you away for a while after the inquest,' she said. 'I was angry at the conclusion, and I took it out on you, and it wasn't your fault, not at all, I know that.' She was mortified to find that tears had come to her eyes. They were unbidden, but nevertheless, she felt she was being dishonest and manipulative.

'Hey,' said John. He picked up a clean serviette from the table and handed it to her. 'I knew you were angry with me about the inquest, and I thought I'd better give you some space. We're all right now, aren't we?'

'I hope so,' said Heather. The tears had receded, so she wiped her mouth with the serviette.

'Except you don't want to go on holiday with me,' he said, 'but I'll let that go for now.'

'It's not that, I told you,' said Heather. She could see he was joking. Or was he? 'Thanks for bringing me to the seaside.'

They went into the light-filled space of the gallery foyer. Heather hooked her arm through John's as they looked at the exhibits there – life-size papier mâché figures in carnival dress. They looked at the programme up on the vast white wall. There were a lot of activities going on in the building for children and adults – painting, drawing, drama – and a varied programme of exhibitions and artistic and musical events. They went up in the lift to look at the collection of Turner paintings. These showed the Margate skies in all their glory and Heather felt like saying, 'See, this is why I'd like to live here, this and this.'

When they left the gallery, they were of one mind and made for the beach. They walked along, close to the edge of the sea, not holding hands, but side by side, under the massive dome of sky that would later redden and explode with colours when the sun went down.

They walked back to the car in the late afternoon. They'd discussed having fish and chips, but neither of them was hungry so they agreed to set off back to London and get a takeaway once they were home.

Progress on the drive back was steady, with just a couple of brief hold-ups. The sun was shining brightly ahead of them and John lowered the visor on his side so he could see the road. Heather found a Bob Dylan CD in the glove compartment and put that on. They talked very little on the way back, sitting in what Heather hoped was a companionable silence. She could almost imagine what it would be like if they were living together, and the warm, safe feeling she might have if they did not have to part and were coming home from a day out to an evening together, to endless days and nights together. But she was acutely aware that she hadn't told him about a lot of things she had done and intended to do. She wondered if it would ever be possible for them to really be together.

John dropped Heather off at her house. He had to take the car back to Claire's because she needed it the following morning. Claire lived in Ealing, and he would get a cab back, he said, and wouldn't be long, but Heather imagined him getting drawn in with Claire and the children, having to do some task Claire required in exchange for the loan of the car, or Claire would want to ask him about this woman he was seeing and taking out for the day and would ply him with tea, or a glass of wine, to keep him there a bit longer.

He called her once he was in a cab and on the way round and she began to relax then and to look forward to the evening with him. He was bringing fish and chips, so she got plates ready, and salt and pepper and vinegar.

He came in looking mellow and handsome and handed her the package of food.

'The cab driver can't have been best pleased at you stinking out his car,' she said, as she tipped the chips onto the plates.

'Oh, he knows me,' said John.

There's a trace of arrogance in him, Heather thought. Why did she find it attractive? And he was so well known in the area. Would she always be able to keep her investigation from him? And did he already know more about her activities than he was letting on?

22

On Monday morning, John went to work, and Heather went to her consulting room at Number 27. She was anxious to make headway in her investigation into what had happened to Phoebe and felt irritable and agitated as she prepared for her first client at ten o'clock. How would she focus? She fantasised about breaking into Phoebe's flat to look for clues. She even imagined breaking in with Martin – she couldn't understand why. Was he not her main suspect? Did she feel some affinity with him, some empathy? Did she fancy him? She winced at the thought. There would be no point in breaking into Phoebe's flat. Apart from the fact that it would be a crime and disastrous for her relationship with John, it was too late; the police forensic team had been in there and dusted for fingerprints and taken stuff away. Anyway, by now there was probably a new tenant in the flat. Stupid fantasy.

The shrill peal of the front doorbell brought her back into the present and she went into the hall to let her client in. For the next fifty minutes, she forced herself to focus on the client and his obsessive compulsive behaviour.

When he'd gone, she made a cafetière of coffee in the kitchen. Mrs Bird came in and wanted to chat. She hadn't spoken to anyone all weekend except the staff in the supermarket, she said.

'Not your son?' Heather asked.

'Oh, yes, he telephoned me,' she said. 'Sunday, eleven o'clock, regular as clockwork.' She sniffed, as if unimpressed by his predictability.

Heather excused herself and went back to her room. She made some notes about the client she'd just seen and found herself looking up from the paper, at the calendar, out of the window, distracted by her own thoughts. She wanted to phone Max, but something was stopping her; something made her think it was not a good idea this time. Usually, she wanted to run things past Max to see what he thought, but this time, no. Why was that? Because he would probably warn her not to do what she was planning to do, and she didn't know how else to proceed. She had to contact Martin and try to meet up with him again. It had to be done. She wanted to know who gave him an alibi and, most importantly, she thought he might know what really happened to Phoebe.

She figured Martin would not be in good shape on a Monday morning, so left it until later. She checked her emails, made a couple of calls, had a sandwich for lunch, saw another client. Mid-afternoon, she called him.

'What do you want?' he said, when he heard her voice. He sounded bleary, even at that time of the day.

'To buy you a drink.'

'What for?'

'There was an inquest hearing into Phoebe's death,' she said. 'I was there. I could tell you about it.'

The mention of the inquest seemed to wake him up. He cleared his throat and asked her where she wanted to meet and when. They agreed to meet on Friday evening in his local pub in Shepherd's Bush, the pub where they'd met soon after the funeral.

She had to get this over with, in order to move on from her obsession with Phoebe. It was getting in the way of her relationship with John, she knew that. She loved him, but the relationship was blighted by this obsession. The only way she could purge herself of it was to find out what happened to Phoebe; she had to solve the mystery, find out where the responsibility lay for her death and get justice for her. Jean wanted this, too. Heather could also see that she needed to absolve herself from blame.

She saw Martin as soon as she entered the pub. He was sitting in the same place as the last time they met there, on a bench seat opposite the door, with the remains of a pint in front of him. He'd shaved off the moustache and beard. His black hair was still quite long, curling on his neck, and he looked more like when she'd first seen him, at Phoebe's funeral. He had on a white T-shirt and his eyes were very green. He was good-looking again. The last time, at the fair, he'd looked thinner, seedier, nervier. It was early evening, and the bar was already quite crowded. She walked over to Martin's table.

'Can I get you another pint?'

He nodded. 'It's cider.'

She went to the bar and ordered his pint and a mineral

water for herself. While she waited for the drinks, she set her phone to record.

Back at the table, she hung her jacket on the back of the seat opposite Martin, sat down and put her phone on the table.

'How are you, Martin?'

'You know, so-so.' His eyes really were a striking green.

'Were you told about the inquest hearing?' she asked.

'No, but they wouldn't tell me,' he said. 'I'm nobody.'

Heather felt sorry for him; whatever he'd done, or not done, he'd lost his girlfriend and had low self-esteem and was probably depressed. She wished she could help him but told herself to snap out of it.

Martin was looking into her eyes. 'Are you going to tell me, then?' he said. 'What happened at the inquest?'

'The coroner listened to evidence from the pathologist, the police, a therapist,' she said, watching his face. 'She considered whether it might have been suicide...'

Martin was shaking his head.

'And the possibility that someone killed her.'

His eyes opened wider for a fraction of a second and he sat forward, waiting for her to continue.

'She decided it was neither of those,' said Heather.

He sat back and his shoulders dropped.

'The coroner concluded that it was an accident,' she said.

'That's right,' said Martin. He coughed. 'It must have been an accident.'

'It sounds as if you know,' said Heather.

'No. How would I know? I just think it must've been

an accident. I don't think Phoebe would've killed herself. And who would've killed her, unless it was a burglar, or some random bloke she had in there. Did they mention me?'

'Yes, the police said they'd talked to you and that you had an alibi for the evening Phoebe died.'

Martin nodded and took a swig of cider.

Heather was silent for a few moments, and then she said, 'There's something bothering me, something I've been wanting to ask you.'

'What's that?'

'Who gave you an alibi for that evening?'

'Oh, not this again!' He slammed his glass down on the table and some of the contents splashed out. 'Why the fuck do you want to know that? What difference does it make?' His face was white, and his eyes flashed with anger, or fear.

'I'm curious, that's all,' she said. 'Why don't you want to say?'

He sighed. 'It was my mate Nick,' he said. 'He told the police I was in here all night. OK, he's a mate, but he still wouldn't want to perjure himself or whatever it is, would he?'

Heather swallowed and felt colour rising in her face.

'What's his surname, this Nick?' she said.

Martin looked upwards, obviously trying to recall. 'Wheeler. It's Nick Wheeler,' he said. 'Why?'

'Oh, nothing,' said Heather, clasping her hands together under the table and trying to appear calm. 'I wondered if I might know him.' She certainly did know him – he was the obsessed client who had stalked her, and who she hoped she would never see again.

'You know Nick?' said Martin.

'No,' she said. 'I thought I might, but no.'

'He comes in here all the time,' said Martin, and he knocked back the last of his cider. 'Are we having another one?'

Heather was having trouble controlling her breathing. She made an effort to breathe deep into her diaphragm.

'I need some air,' she said. 'It's really stuffy in here.'

Now Martin was studying her face. 'We could go outside for a smoke,' he said.

'Look,' she said. 'Could we go somewhere else? I could do with a walk as well.'

'We could go back to my place,' said Martin. 'It's not far. If you want to risk it.' He smiled his stunning smile.

'Yes, OK,' she said. She picked up her phone, switched off recording and put it in her bag. She knew she may have looked too keen, but she wanted to get out of there and she'd been hoping to get Martin on his own, so this served her purpose well.

They walked along the main road a little way. Martin called into an off-licence and bought some cider and cigarettes. Heather waited in the shop and the man behind the counter looked at her with curiosity. It brought back memories of her drinking days, buying booze to take home, often in the company of a man.

A few yards on they turned into a side road lined with tall terraced houses, all converted into flats. They turned left, and Martin took out a key and opened the front door of one of the houses. Heather followed him in and up to the first floor. He showed her into his sitting room. It contained a scruffy, grey three-seater settee and a coffee table with two overflowing ashtrays and an empty glass on it and ring marks where glasses and mugs had been set down. There was not much else in the room, just a television, a sound system on a small bookcase and two guitars leaning against the wall opposite the settee. A poster of Jimi Hendrix had pride of place on the wall. The carpet was thin and of an indeterminate dark colour.

Heather was intensely aware of the intimacy of the situation, of being in this young man's space. Martin stood a foot from her, with his carrier bag of cider. She could see his chest moving as he breathed. She moved to the window and looked out at the street. It was dusk and a new moon was rising in the clear sky over the houses opposite.

'What can I get you to drink?' said Martin. 'I've got lemonade if you want.'

Heather turned and faced him again.

'I'll join you in a glass of cider,' she said. *It can't hurt*, she thought. *One glass of cider can't hurt.*

Martin went along the passage and came back with two glasses and a bottle of Strongbow cider with condensation on it, cold from the fridge.

Heather sat on the settee and watched as Martin unscrewed the top of the bottle. It came off with a hiss. He poured the golden, bubbly liquid into the glasses and handed one to her. She put the glass on the table. Martin sat down next to her, lit a cigarette and offered her one. She took it and leant towards him to light it from the flame of his lighter. She took a puff and coughed; the last time she'd smoked was after Phoebe's funeral and it had been one of Martin's cigarettes that time as well. She picked up the glass of cider and took a sip. That lovely fresh taste of apple! She'd dreamt of it, over the years. More than once, walking in the street on a blazing hot summer's day, she'd imagined walking into a pub, ordering a half of cider and drinking it down. She took a bigger sip, and another, and had a drag on her cigarette. She'd dreamt of smoking too. She used to enjoy smoking; if it were not so harmful, she wouldn't have stopped. She felt a bit light-headed and anxious. The cure for that was more cider, so she drank what was left in the glass.

Martin was watching her, a half-smile on his face. He refilled her glass.

'It's refreshing,' she said. 'I'd forgotten.'

She drank some more cider and felt a warmth filling her stomach, warming the anxiety away.

'I'd forgotten what I was missing,' she said.

'Yeah?'

She leant her head back and the warmth spread to her chest. Slightly dizzy, she straightened her head.

'I need a piss,' said Martin and he left the room.

Heather remembered she wanted to record. She fumbled in her bag for her phone, brought it near her face to look at it and set it to record. She took off her jacket, put the phone in the pocket and put the jacket over the settee arm. She felt like giggling. What the hell was she doing? This was mad. She heard the toilet flush, and Martin appeared in the doorway.

'What's so funny?' he said.

He sat closer to her this time. Their knees were almost touching.

'This situation,' she said. 'Me, here, in your place.'

'What's funny about that?' he said. 'If you want a laugh, how about some weed?'

'Oh, I don't think so, but you go ahead if you want.'

He broke up a cigarette and made a joint with some grass he had in his pocket. He lit it and Heather found she was breathing the smoke in deeply, enjoying the old familiar smell.

'Go on, then,' she said, and took the joint when he offered it.

She took a draw, and it made her cough and feel dizzy, so she handed it back. She'd stopped using weed because it made her paranoid and that was the last thing she wanted to feel now. She drank some cider, and it soothed her throat.

'Well, well, well,' said Martin. 'The ice queen is melting, I think.'

He put his arm along the back of the settee behind her, leant towards her and kissed her on the mouth. She returned his kiss and felt herself swooning, backwards and down, her stomach swooping as it had on the fairground ride.

He pulled away and looked into her eyes.

'What is it about you?' he said.

He kissed her again, a shorter kiss this time.

'You remind me of Phoebe,' he said, his cheek next to hers. His hair was soft and smelled of shampoo.

'Really?' She put her arms around him and drew him closer.

'Yes, I don't know what it is,' he said, 'but you do.'

'I knew her, so I'm a connection with her, I suppose.'

'It's more than that,' he said.

Heather felt strange, as if the boundaries of her identity were blurring and she might be Phoebe, falling under Martin's spell. She heard herself make a sound, a low moan. She cleared her throat and moved slightly away from Martin; their arms were still around each other.

'What's the matter?' he said.

'I feel a bit strange. Not used to drinking.'

He touched her breast, and she let him. She liked him touching her. *This is wrong*, she thought. *Do I want this?* She searched for John in her mind and found him, looking intently at her, the way he did when he was thinking, trying to work things out.

Martin removed his hand from her breast and picked up the joint from the ashtray. He took a draw on it and offered it to Heather. She shook her head. He breathed out the smoke.

'Did you fancy Phoebe?' he said.

'No,' she said. 'She reminded me of myself when I was younger.'

He laughed. 'There, you see. That's so weird.'

He poured more cider into both their glasses, took a drink from his own and topped it up, and then he turned to her, his face serious.

'Did you love her? I loved her so much,' he said. 'I told her, nobody will ever love you like I do.'

He was becoming maudlin and perhaps this was good – it might make him more likely to open up.

'It must have hurt you terribly when she finished the relationship,' she said.

'What do you think?' He looked sidelong at her, a wild look in his eyes.

She felt vaguely alarmed. She reached out and laid her hand on his forearm; it was firm, the muscles tense. She remembered Phoebe talking about making up with Martin after he'd been violent towards her, the first time. He'd kicked her on the shin. Phoebe had known she should end the relationship, but she was in love with him by then: *'His smell and his body were so familiar, the feel of his arm when I put my hand on it.'*

Martin was speaking. Heather tuned back in to him.

'I kept going round there because I thought she might be seeing someone else,' he said. 'I wanted to know if she was seeing anyone.'

'What would you have done if you'd caught her with another man?'

She sensed something hovering on the periphery of her consciousness, a realisation coming, something new that could change everything.

Martin was shaking his head.

'Would you have wanted to kill him?' she asked.

'Not him, no.' He sounded impatient.

She removed her hand from his arm and turned her whole body towards him. 'You would have killed Phoebe?' she said, more loudly than she'd intended.

'No,' he said, his voice almost a whine. 'I would've killed myself. I told her that. She had to take me back or I would kill myself.'

He was looking so downcast, a part of Heather wanted to put her arms around him and comfort him, but at the same time she was sickened by his self-pity and angry at the emotional blackmail he had subjected Phoebe to. Did he have no inkling that this was what it was?

'You can't make someone love you like that,' she said.

He flinched as if struck. 'And now she's gone and it's my fault.' He covered his face with his hands.

'What do you mean?'

'I never meant it to happen, but it did and it's down to me.'

'What do you mean? Tell me what happened.'

He dropped his hands, and she saw that his face was contorted.

'That night, I'd been drinking vodka,' he said. 'I went round there, and she let me come up. She said again that we were finished.' He stopped and hunched his shoulders.

'Go on,' she said. 'What happened?'

'I told her I'd kill myself if she kept pushing me away and she didn't believe me, so I went out on the balcony, and she came after me. I really meant to do it; I wasn't pretending. I'd had enough. I had one leg over the railing, and she was screaming at me to stop it, and I swung the other leg up and I was balancing, and I nearly fell and she leant over and started pulling me and I got my legs back over but somehow she lost her balance, and she fell.'

Heather remembered then. She'd forgotten and now she remembered. In one of their sessions, Phoebe had told her that Martin had said he didn't want to live without her, and she was afraid he "*might do something to himself*". In all this time, throughout her investigation and the inquest, this was a scenario she'd never imagined.

She stared at him.

'I'm in hell,' he said, 'if that's any consolation.'

'It's not. I should tell the police.'

'Why? It was an accident, like they said at the inquest.'

He moved closer to her and tried to kiss her again. She turned her face away at first, and then let him kiss her. The falling feeling she had this time was much more to do with alcohol consumption than lust. She pulled away.

'No, I can't do this!' she said. Somehow she got to her feet.

A phone was ringing, and she realised it was her own. Her jacket had dropped onto the floor. She picked it up, found the pocket and her phone. It was John calling. In a second, Martin was on his feet and grabbing the phone from her hand. She tried to keep hold of it and to push him away, but he was stronger, and he took it with one hand and held her back with the other. He looked at it and then threw it against the wall and the hard case fell off. She rushed over and picked up the phone and case, grabbed her jacket and bag and headed for the door. Martin stood in the doorway, his arms out, barring her way.

'Where are you going?' he said, the wild look in his eyes again.

'I'm going home,' she said. Her heart was beating fast. 'Who's John?'

'A friend. Come on, Martin. I want to go home.'

He moved to one side, and she walked past him, opened the door to the staircase and stepped out of the flat.

'What are you going to do?' he yelled after her.

She closed the door and ran down the stairs and out into the street. She walked to the end of the road and looked around, disorientated; she could see the lights and traffic of the main road off to the right, so she went that way, breathing deeply, aware that she was unsteady on her legs.

It was still busy on the main road that late into the evening. A lot of people were out on the street: groups of young Somali men, older men, women in short skirts, women in hijabs. Heather weaved between the people, trying not to bump into them. Banks of fruit and vegetables were displayed outside wide shop fronts with Arabic script above the windows. Drivers of cars and black cabs hooted their horns; a bus purred by, giving off a blast of warm air; youngsters careered by on bicycles.

She reached the underground station, went inside and swiped her Oyster. Her priority was to get out of Shepherd's Bush. She could get a train to Hammersmith and a bus or taxi from there. As she waited on the platform, she began to shiver, so she turned up the collar of her thin jacket and hunched her shoulders. Martin's words were in her ears. What was she going to do? She would tell John, that's what she would do. That's what she had to do. She had new evidence so they could challenge the inquest verdict, maybe reopen the case. The train drew in and she stepped into the bright carriage, relieved to be with people, even if most of them were looking at their phones. She sat and took her own phone out of her bag. The glass was smashed; it had a chip out of it and cracks radiating out. Was it still working? There was a text, John asking her to give him a call. She would do that, she definitely would, but not now.

In Hammersmith, she came out onto the busy Broadway, crossed the road and walked round the corner into a Wetherspoon's pub. She made her way across what seemed like a vast expanse of uneven floor to the bar. She'd been in there a couple of times years ago, but no-one was likely to know her. She felt herself swaying slightly and rested her forearms on the counter. She ordered a large white wine, her old tipple.

'All right, darlin'?' It was a scruffy, red-faced old man propping up the bar nearby, a leering expression on his face that said, *How about it, then?* She looked at the other men at the bar and she seemed to be surrounded by leering faces. She grabbed her drink, made for a table and plonked herself on a chair. She closed her eyes for a moment, thinking, *no-one knows I'm here.* Relief. She took a sip of the cold wine and savoured its fruity taste, knowing it would anaesthetise her eventually. If this one glass didn't do the trick, she would get herself another. She didn't care. *I've got you now, Martin*, she thought. Or had she? She took out her phone. If the text function was working, hopefully the recording would still be on there. She couldn't play it now. She just needed to calm down. Relax. Another sip of wine. Martin was so volatile; she felt she had done well to get away from him with only her phone screen smashed. *Well, Phoebe, I know now what he's like and what happened to you. I should tell the police straight away so they can pick him up.* She took another sip of wine. Jean would be so grateful to her for finding out the truth. Alan could just back off, no need for any more hostility from him. She wanted to see John, but best not contact him right now. *Sorry, John, I let him kiss me. It was necessary, to get him to open up.* Something about entrapment came into her mind. Could it be construed as entrapment? No, more of a honey trap, that was it. Honey trap. Max would know. Her finger was poised over her phone keyboard. *No. Call*

Max when you get home. She finished her wine and went to the bar for a refill.

She didn't care now about the leering faces. She smiled graciously at them and at the young barman who served her.

'Let me get that.' The man addressing her was a younger, more attractive version of the red-faced man who had spoken to her earlier. This one had bright-blue eyes and white teeth.

'If you insist,' she said.

'I do.' He took a twenty pound note from a wad and handed it to the barman.

'Thank you,' she said. 'I need to sit down, though. Stuff to think about.'

He indicated the seating area. 'Be my guest.'

She took her drink and returned to her table. The man's blue eyes were on her. She smiled at him and raised her glass.

23

She woke up with a start. What day was it? She'd had a deep, dreamless sleep and felt bleary, thick-headed. She reached for her clock. Ten past eight. It was Saturday, wasn't it? Thank goodness. She let her head drop back onto the pillow, turned the pillow cool side up and flopped down again. On no, what had she done? She lay on her back and the room began to spin, so she turned back on to her side and swung her legs out from under the duvet. Gingerly, she sat up on the side of the bed and looked down at herself; at least she had her pyjamas on. Her clothes were in a messy heap on the chair, not piled neatly as they would usually be. Her mouth was dry and tasted foul. Ah, she'd had the foresight to put a glass of water on the bedside table; she picked it up, hand shaking, and drank it down. What the hell had happened? It was coming back to her in bursts, like short trailers from a film – Martin opening a bottle of cider and pouring it, the half-smile on his face as she drank it, him kissing her and then his contorted face before he blurted out what had happened to Phoebe. There was a tussle over her phone, and he'd thrown it and then he'd tried to stop her leaving and had yelled after her, 'What are you going to do?' She remembered staggering to the station, buying a glass of wine in the pub, the leering faces, the man with the blue eyes and wad of notes who bought her second drink, raising her glass to him. And then? What happened then?

She stood up and her head was throbbing. She walked unsteadily to the door and onto the landing, one hand on the wall to keep her balance and, carefully, she walked down the stairs. She could hardly see. Had the alcohol brought on a migraine? No, this was a just a hangover. She reached the kitchen and put the kettle on. Paracetamol. There should be some. She pulled cough mixture, plasters and tubes of cream out of the medicine cupboard, found a pack of paracetamol and swallowed two tablets with water. Her hand shook so much as she spooned coffee into the cafetière that a lot of it spilled on the work surface.

She waited for the coffee to brew. A taxi. That was it. A black cab. She'd chatted and laughed with the driver. She was alone in the back, she was sure. Thank God. Why had she let that dreadful man buy her drinks? He'd bought her more than one, hadn't he? It was like a horrible flashback to the past, but it had actually happened last night.

She sat in an armchair in the sitting room, with her coffee, and cringed to think how she'd behaved and what might have happened, what she would have been capable of, because she knew she might have got off with that man; it was probably touch and go.

'No, I wouldn't have,' she said, aloud. 'I'm not slipping back into that. No.'

The headache was receding, but she felt sick, queasy.

She couldn't face eating anything. The coffee might not be helping, but she wanted it – the smell of it reassured her that she was not drinking alcohol this morning and life just might go on. At times in the past, after a bender, if she'd felt this bad in the morning she would've opened a bottle of wine, or most likely there would be one open from the night before, left out of the fridge, so it would be warm and stale, but she would slug it back and stop shaking and the world would start to seem funny and friendly, and she would soon be ready to venture out to a café for breakfast, or go straight to the pub.

In a way, she was nostalgic for those days when she'd given herself up to alcohol, but she knew there was a price to be paid, and she had not stayed sober for all these years, gained some self-esteem and built a career, only to wreck it all now for the pleasure of getting off her face. It stopped here. Luckily, there was no alcohol in the house. Was there? No, she was pretty sure there was no alcohol, except Chanel No 5 – she recalled having a bottle of it confiscated when she entered the detox unit – and she was not about to drink that. She was thankful that an obstacle stood in the way of her obtaining any alcohol, for to get it she would have to go to a shop and that, at present, was out of the question – she was too shaky and queasy. Nowadays she had too much self-respect to let herself be seen in this state. She would get through it.

Anxiety and relief came in waves. Anxiety rushed in when she thought about the fact that she'd been drinking, a lot. And then relief that she'd got home, and she was alone and had two days to recover. She could put a stop to it now and prevent this lapse from becoming a complete relapse. Anxiety surged up when she thought about kissing Martin. If she told John, how would he take it? Would he finish the relationship? If she didn't tell him, it would be a secret she would have to keep and that could affect the relationship. And it wouldn't be the only thing she was keeping from him. She was already deceiving him; she hadn't told him about visiting the off-licence near Phoebe's flat, her meetings with Martin and the most recent developments with Jean and Alan. If she told him what she now knew about Phoebe's death, she would have to tell him about kissing Martin, because Martin might tell and that would be worse.

Relief washed over her when she recalled that she now knew she could not have foreseen or prevented Phoebe's death. It had been Martin's fault that Phoebe fell. She, Heather, was not in any way to blame. She'd helped Phoebe to make sense of her patterns of behaviour and to value herself more. Whilst in therapy, Phoebe had reduced her drinking, started a job she enjoyed and ended the abusive relationship with Martin. As a therapist, she was not responsible for the fact that Martin was unable to accept that the relationship was over; Phoebe had been her client, not Martin. What could she do with this knowledge? Was it enough just to know she was not to blame? She could tell John and perhaps he would take it forward and there would be justice for Phoebe, and for her mother, Jean. But if she told John, he would probably never forgive her for doubting his professional judgement, going against his wishes and undermining his professional reputation, because that was what she'd done; she'd shown that he had not investigated Phoebe's death thoroughly, and he hadn't got to the truth; he had abandoned the case prematurely. Even if this was understandable due to time and work pressures, it showed him in a bad light. No, he would not forgive her. Anxiety flooded back in, and she felt her shoulders caving.

Perhaps she should check her evidence. Whether she had evidence would inform her decisions about who and what to tell. Where was her phone? She looked around. It must be upstairs in her bag. She stood and pain shot through her temples. She climbed the stairs, slowly, almost on her knees, using the banister to haul herself up. The bag was next to her bed. She felt in it and was relieved to find the phone was there. She drew it out and winced at the sight of the smashed screen. So that had really happened; Martin had really thrown it against the wall. She took a deep breath, found the recording and played it back. The pub conversation was clearly audible. In the recording done in the flat, the voices were muffled. She turned up the volume and it was possible to make out what was said: '*What's funny about that?*' Martin's voice. She moved it on. Her own voice: '*I feel a bit strange. Not used to drinking.*' It was possible to catch most of it. Martin's account of the night Phoebe died was there, muffled, but just about audible. And then there was a dull thud, and the recording stopped. Ah, yes. The jacket had dropped onto the floor and the phone had started ringing – John calling.

As if on cue, the ring tone started now. Heather's whole body jerked, and she nearly dropped the phone. It was John. She was tempted to let it go to voicemail, but she answered the call.

'Are you all right?' he said.

The sound of his voice made her want to cry.

'Yes, I'm sorry I didn't call you back.' She didn't want him to know she'd been drinking, not right now anyway. 'I was with a friend last night and it got late.'

'Oh,' he said. The line was silent for a moment. 'Late would have been OK. Or a text. But you're OK anyway, that's the main thing. Do you want to do something later?'

'Actually, I'm not feeling too good this morning. A bit queasy. We had this takeaway Chinese. I don't know if it was that, but anyway, can we leave it today, please. Sorry.'

'Tomorrow, then? I'm free in the evening. Shall I pick you up at seven? We can have dinner. If you've recovered, that is.'

Was he being sarcastic? It wasn't like him to be sarcastic. Did he suspect something was amiss, that she was not telling him the truth? After the call, Heather flopped backwards onto the bed and tears ran from the corners of her eyes. She wanted to tell John everything, absolutely everything. She knew it might kill their relationship, but what was the point of the relationship if there was so much deceit? If they were to be together, they had to be honest with each other, surely? Well, that was what she had always believed. Her head still didn't like this position, and the room began to spin again. She sat up, reached for a tissue and wiped her eyes and blew her nose. Max. She needed Max. He would be up. She would call him. First of all, she needed water. Plenty of water was the key to recovery. Water and time. She hoped that by the time she saw John the following evening, she would feel more like herself and would know how much she wanted to tell him.

She went downstairs, filled a pint glass with water and took it into the sitting room. She sat in her armchair and found Max in her list of contacts. The call went to voicemail. She left a message asking him to call her. She felt bereft, alone and very unwell. She arranged cushions at one end of the settee and curled up on it with her head on the cushions, her knees pulled up to her chest. It was sunny outside, and birds were singing. She loved the sound of the birds singing at dawn and when she'd had trouble sleeping in the past, she'd always been able to drift off once they started their dawn chorus. She drifted off now, in and out of a doze. How pathetic to be napping like this, in the morning, but never mind. *Be kind to yourself*, she thought, *as you want your clients to be. As you wanted Phoebe to be. Poor Martin*, she thought, *poor Martin, living with the knowledge of what he has done.* How would she make John understand that she had to know what happened to Phoebe? A dream began: John looking sad, Martin was there as well; it was unclear where they were; Martin shouting. Her phone was ringing, and she woke, and it really was ringing. She sat up and reached for it.

'Max?'

'Hiya. What's up? You sounded like it was something urgent.'

'Did I? Oh, sorry. It's just... Max, I was drinking last night, and I feel really bad.'

'Ach, that's not good news, hen. I'm speaking from a position of moral superiority here, you understand, being as sober as a judge. Can you get back on the wagon, pronto?'

'That's my plan, yes. I haven't had any alcohol this

morning.' She reached for her glass of water and took several large sips.

'That's something, anyway. Do you know what triggered it?'

'Oh, yes.'

'Well, come on. Spill.'

She told Max about meeting Martin in the pub and finding out Nick had been the one who gave Martin an alibi, wanting to get out of the pub in case he came in and ending up in Martin's flat. She stopped, waited for him to say something.

'What happened?' he said, eventually.

She gave him an account of what she could remember happening in the flat and then in the pub and her virtual blackout about the end of the evening and getting home.

'Phew!' he said. 'You don't do things by halves, do you?'

'I don't know how much to tell John, if anything.'

'I can see that you wouldn't.'

She'd hoped he would have some advice for her, as he usually did. But she couldn't expect him to tell her what to do. She could rely on him to give her information and point out what to look for, or that she'd missed something. She drank some more water.

'One thing I was wondering,' she said. 'Would there be anything the police or the coroner could do if they had this information and the recording as evidence?'

'Sure,' he said. 'Martin could be charged with involuntary manslaughter. Phoebe died because of his reckless behaviour. It can carry a prison sentence.'

After the conversation with Max, she took a shower. It

was a huge effort, but as she dried her hair in the bedroom, she felt a lot better. She put on jeans and a shirt and went down to the kitchen. There was a tin of chicken soup at the back of a cupboard, so she had the soup for lunch, with some toast, and put on the radio. She tried to listen to a news programme but found it difficult to concentrate. She kept thinking about Martin, imagined him in a police cell under arrest, possibly remanded to prison, in the dock in a criminal court and then serving a prison sentence. How would his mental health stand up to all that? She would be responsible for putting him through it.

And then she recalled what Max had said at the end of their conversation: '*You need to think through the possible consequences for you and your career. And remember, he might not go down. He might be acquitted.*' She would have to attend court and be cross-examined, and she would be pulled apart by his defence counsel, all her subterfuge exposed, her character shredded. Was she ready for that? It could be the end of her career. The sad face of John from her dream that morning came back to her. On the other hand, if she didn't act on the information, what would she tell Jean and Alan? Heather had set off on this mission alone and then Jean had begged her to continue with it and find out what had happened to Phoebe. How could she keep the truth from Jean?

The afternoon crept by, punctuated by glasses of water and cups of tea, accompanied by old episodes of *Poirot* and *Morse* on the television. She made herself eat some fish at dinner time. Good for the brain? She hoped so. In the evening, she watched more television – annoying quiz shows, a silly comedy, a depressing film – waiting for it to get dark, and then dozing, until it seemed reasonable to go to bed. It took her a long time to get to sleep, thoughts going round and round in her head. She slept fitfully, awoke at dawn, and birdsong lulled her into a more restful sleep.

John picked her up at seven that evening as promised. She'd spent the day doing washing and housework and a bit of gardening. She had almost recovered, but not quite. She made an effort to look good, putting on eye make-up and a dress and jacket – it was to make herself feel better as much as anything, because she still felt weak and a bit shaky. John was in his Mondeo this time. She felt he was scrutinising her as she climbed into the passenger seat. She smiled and leant over and kissed his cheek.

'You all right today?' he asked.

'Yes, thanks,' she said. 'I'm starving.'

He turned on the ignition and pulled away. 'Glad to hear it. Italian OK?'

Heather had ordered prawn linguine and was struggling to finish it. She glanced at the glasses of wine on the next table and wished she could have one.

'I thought you were starving,' said John, cutting into his steak. He was drinking a beer and the smell of it was hoppy and pungent.

'I thought I was,' she said.

'Look, is something the matter?' he said. 'Are we OK?'

'Yes, I hope we are. Aren't we? I…' She almost said "I love you" and stopped herself because she knew it would sound desperate if she said it now and she didn't want that.

'Something is bothering you,' he said.

Heather gripped the napkin on her lap, apprehensive about what might be coming, what he might say next and, also, what she might say herself.

'Are you still troubled about Phoebe's death?' he said.

Heather breathed out through her mouth. 'I can honestly say that I've stopped blaming myself for Phoebe's death,' she said. 'I couldn't have prevented it; I know that now.'

'I'm pleased to hear it. I told you there was no way you were to blame. What convinced you, finally?'

She closed her eyes and shook her head. 'John, there's something I have to tell you.' She opened her eyes and looked across the table at his handsome, serious face. 'On Friday night, I had a drink,' she said. 'Well, more than one. I had a lot of drinks. I was pissed and I needed the weekend to recover.'

'Shit. That was after how long?'

'I've stopped. I've got no intention of carrying on drinking.'

'I wouldn't have had this beer if I'd known.' He moved the glass further away from her.

'You must carry on as normal,' she said.

She heard her phone bleep. Her bag was between her feet. She reached down and took the phone out. It was just a text from the phone company.

'Sorry, I always feel I have to check in case it's about Dad.' She slid the phone back into her bag.

'What happened to the screen?' said John.

'I dropped it on Friday night,' she said. 'I suppose I could take it to one of those repair shops.'

'I suppose you could,' said John.

He looked at her for a long time and she felt sure he suspected there was more to it, that she was keeping something from him.

24

By the time Heather went to work at work at Number 27 on Monday morning, she was feeling stronger, but she was still quite anxious. John hadn't pushed her about the smashed phone screen, not yet anyway. She couldn't believe he would leave it there, as he was attuned to picking up lies and implausibilities; it was his job. He was also good at biding his time. He'd been quiet during the rest of the evening. That night, she'd welcomed the closeness of his body, but she felt guilty; she felt that she didn't deserve to be with him.

While she was with her obsessive-compulsive client, she was aware that her own anxiety was interfering with the way she related to him. She did her best to be calm and containing. Afterwards, she made coffee and chatted briefly to Mrs Bird before returning to her room. She was making notes when she heard the ping of a text arriving. It was from Martin: *Need to see you. Call me.* Of course. He had her number because she'd called him, several times. She was so used to initiating contact with him, she hadn't thought about him contacting her. Her anxiety level shot up. She sent a reply, saying she was at work and would call him that evening. All day it kept coming back into her mind that she had to face speaking to Martin later. She wondered if he would tell anyone about their evening together.

She was home just after six and wanted to get the phone call over with, so she made tea and sat down to make the call. Now, when she looked at the smashed phone screen, she felt angry with Martin. She composed herself and called him.

He said, 'When can I see you?'

Hell, he doesn't waste time, she thought. Perhaps he can't tolerate waiting.

'I'm not sure that's a good idea,' she said.

'What? I like you. I want to see you.'

Alarm bells were ringing. Heather knew she'd brought this upon herself; she'd encouraged it.

'I'm too old for you, Martin,' she said. She winced as she recalled saying a similar thing to Nick when he'd followed her into the café.

'I don't care,' he said. 'You weren't too old for me on Friday, were you?'

'Yes, I deserve that,' she said, 'and I'm sorry. I've stopped drinking again. I've got work.' She reminded herself that Martin didn't know she was a therapist.

'Well, good for you,' he said.

He was silent. She could hear him breathing. And then he said, 'Have you told anyone about our conversation? About Phoebe?'

'No, I haven't.'

'Are you going to tell anyone?'

'I don't know.'

'God, you'd better not tell anyone!' His voice got louder, his tone more desperate. 'I'm going mad here, wondering what's going to happen. I'm wondering whether the police are coming for me.'

Her turn to be silent. Her breathing was fast and shallow. She wondered if he could hear it.

After a moment, he said, 'Well, say something.'

'Have you told anyone else how she died?'

'No.' He laughed. 'I wish I hadn't told you.'

'Why did you?'

'It was eating away at me, man,' he said. 'Still is.'

Silence again.

'Can't we meet?' he said.

'I'm with someone.'

'Is his name John?'

'Yes.'

The line went dead. Heather decided she must tell John what she knew and how she had found out. Martin was a loose cannon. How would he deal with the knowledge that someone knew he was culpable? She should probably tell John before telling Jean; she wanted John to find out from her, and not via some roundabout route.

The next day, Heather was at the therapy centre. She passed through reception and nodded to Maria, who responded with a tight little smile. She reached her consulting room and breathed a sigh of relief; it was a place of relative sanctuary, where there was a good chance she could be calm and think clearly. Today, as she stood by the window, looking at the lush green of the trees and grass in the square, it occurred to her that there was no longer any need to look at Phoebe's session notes whenever she had a spare moment. When she'd been sober for a while and had processed the information she now had about Phoebe's death, perhaps her obsession would fade away, her mind would work better, and she could bring a new clarity and empathy to her work. Maybe she would build her private practice and write papers and articles again. It was not happening yet, for she realised that she didn't just feel guilty about deceiving John; there was still a tinge of guilt left in relation to Phoebe. Why was that?

It became clearer to her during a session with David. He'd made a lot of progress in the past few months. He'd found a new job, was not bingeing and was spending less time with his mother. He was more assertive. The trouble was, his marriage was not going at all well. He'd mentioned before that he and his wife were having a lot of arguments and he talked about this again in the session that day.

'We hardly ever used to argue,' he said. 'I suppose I say what I think more than I used to, and she doesn't always like it.'

'What kind of things are you arguing about?'

'Oh, I don't know. Where to go on holiday, who empties the washing machine, what to buy when we're out shopping, whether we go and see my mother. Brexit, for God's sake. We seem to argue about everything.'

Heather said David had made many positive changes and had grown and changed as a person; this was often difficult for other people, who may feel threatened and resent it. They had discussed this in previous sessions.

'And do you know what she does to end an argument? She closes down on me,' he said. 'Her face kind of closes and she looks really angry and ugly, and she'll walk off and leave me to stew.'

Heather said how difficult that must be.

'That's not all,' he said. 'She won't let me come near her at night. She's either on the far side of the bed or in the spare room. I never thought I'd be talking about this, but our sex life is non-existent now. She's probably going to leave me. And that's down to you!'

Heather had never seen him so angry; she'd never seen him angry at all.

'If I hadn't come here,' he said, 'if I hadn't had this so-called therapy, this wouldn't be happening. We were OK, you know? She was the boss, but it was OK. We loved each other. We knew where we were.'

Afterwards, the word *iatrogenic* came into Heather's mind. It was used when referring to illness caused by medical treatment and David had been talking about the psychotherapeutic equivalent: the side effects or downside of changes achieved during therapy. He'd said "And that's down to you!" with such vehemence and at the time it had hit her like a bolt of bad news and gone straight to her guts. Her cheeks had grown hot, and she'd felt flustered for a several minutes; she'd had to concentrate hard on what David was saying in order to keep her focus. As she made her notes, she tried to recall and record his exact words: '...*it was OK. We loved each other. We knew where we were.*' Phoebe and Martin had loved each other. Maybe they knew where they were before Heather supported her to break away from him. But it had been an abusive relationship, another in a series of abusive relationships for Phoebe. She and Martin were not OK and she needed to make changes in her life. Nevertheless, the fact remained: Heather had helped Phoebe, and she had ended up dead. Heather dropped her head onto her arms on the desk.

That evening, her phone rang just after eight o'clock. She hoped it wasn't Martin, and as she picked it up, she thought, *why don't I get this screen fixed?* It was Jean. This was really inconvenient, and Heather was not prepared for it. However, it was not surprising; they hadn't been in touch for a while and Jean was bound to be impatient for news. Heather took the call.

'Hello, Jean. How are you?'

'I've been quite down, to be honest,' said Jean. Her voice was flat, toneless. 'Do you have anything for me?'

Heather had to think quickly. 'Are you on your own? Is Alan with you?'

'No, he's not here,' Jean replied. 'I thought it best.'

'Good,' said Heather. 'I do have something to tell you, but I want to tell you in person, not over the phone.'

'What is it? Do you know what happened to Phoebe?'

'I want to tell you in person.'

'I can come over, or meet you somewhere, wherever you like.'

'Is it possible,' said Heather, 'to see you on your own, without Alan?'

'Of course, yes.'

'I can come over there, but it'll have to be at the weekend,' said Heather.

'Really? Can't we meet before that?'

'I'm sorry, Jean. There's something I have to do before I see you. I'll explain when we meet.'

The next day, she went to a mobile phone shop after work and bought herself a new phone. In the evening, whilst half watching the television, she transferred her contacts to the new device. She had a new telephone number and could choose who to give it to; she would not give it to Martin. She texted John, asking him if he could meet her outside a pub by the river in Hammersmith the following evening and to please note her new number.

She came back from the kitchen after washing the dishes and found his text. It would be difficult for him to get away tomorrow. He would be free on Saturday. She replied that she was busy on Saturday, and it was important, adding, *I could come to the station if that's easier.* He called her straight away.

'What's the urgency? Are you all right?'

'Yes,' she said. 'I haven't been drinking or anything. I have some things to tell you and... well, it involves a police matter, and I don't want to tell you over the phone.'

'OK. Do you want me to come round? I can rearrange some stuff and get over there by ten.'

She thought for a moment. She wanted to see him, but she didn't want to be rushed and felt it would be better to meet on neutral ground.

'It can wait until tomorrow,' she said.

'Heather, is this about Phoebe?'

'Yes.'

She heard him sigh. 'Tomorrow, then,' he said.

'Thank you.'

Since the session with David, she'd been questioning whether she wanted to continue working as a therapist. Clients had been angry with her before, but David's accusation, coming at that time, had hit a nerve. She'd read a book once about depression in which the author proposed that people were at the mercy of proximal power and distal power and that therapists and managers were mediators between people and the distal power of the system. Was she helping people to fit in better with an inequitable and oppressive system, helping them to adjust? *Do not adjust your mind; there is a fault in reality.* That had been a popular saying at one time, a joke that was deadly serious. What about distress, though? Was it not worthwhile to help people to feel better about themselves and experience less distress and pain? But what if she was causing distress and pain in the process? In a cost-benefit analysis, would she be found to be doing more good than harm, or more harm than good?

There was one damage limitation action she could take, right now. She picked up her old phone with the smashed screen and deleted the recordings of her conversations with Martin.

It was a fine evening as Heather waited on the river walk. She'd bought a lemonade from a pub and was leaning on the wall, looking at the water. It was high tide and ducks paddled and preened near the edge. To the east was the green and gold splendour of Hammersmith Bridge and to the west, a crowd of bobbing houseboats, various sizes and in various states of dilapidation, some with geraniums and other plants on board, giving the effect of a floating garden. On the opposite bank, the trees of Barnes were in full leaf. The sky was blue with a few fluffy clouds.

She felt John's presence before she saw him, his body warmth next to her, his arm briefly around her shoulders in greeting. She looked at his face; the sun was on it, making him squint.

'Why here?' he asked.

'I like it here,' she said. 'I haven't been by the river for a while. Do you want to get yourself a beer?'

'I've got to go back to work so I think I'll get a coffee.'

He went into the pub. A boat crew sped by; a shout from the coxswain startled Heather momentarily. She turned and leant her back against the wall. The tables outside the pub were already filled with early evening drinkers.

John returned with a cup of coffee and asked her if she wanted to find a seat. She said she preferred to stand, where they were, away from the tables.

'You got a new phone, then?' he said.

'Yeah, I needed an upgrade so I thought I might as well.'

He was holding the saucer in one hand and the cup in the other. He took a sip, looked around, and placed the coffee on a step behind him by the wall.

'Are you going to tell me what happened to your phone?' he said. 'You can't have just dropped it.'

'No,' she said. 'It was thrown against a wall.'

'By whom?'

'I think I'd better tell you from the beginning,' she said.

He raised his eyebrows and then nodded. He was looking straight into her face.

'I hadn't known you long,' she said. 'It was the night we went to opera. You told me that a shopkeeper had called the ambulance for Phoebe, and I got it into my head that I had to go and talk to him. Yes, I know I shouldn't have, or I should've told you, but I didn't think you'd be too pleased about it. I went to the shop and spoke to the shopkeeper. He told me that a young man had been in there that night, and he sounded very much like Martin, Phoebe's ex.'

John was frowning.

'You knew I wanted to contact Martin and see what I could find out. I told you and you advised me not to, but I did contact him; in fact, I've seen him several times and each time I felt I was getting closer to finding out what happened to Phoebe. I was torn; sometimes I wanted to drop it and sometimes I felt I had to carry on searching for answers.'

Her mouth was dry. She picked up her glass of lemonade from the ground and drank some of it.

'After the inquest hearing, Phoebe's mother Jean came to see me with her partner, Alan. They turned up, out of the blue. They had my address because I'd given it to them before.' Her cheeks were burning; there was so much to tell, so much she'd kept from him. 'Anyway, Jean was devastated by the inquest conclusion, and she asked me to see what I could find out. They had worked out that I was the therapist mentioned by the coroner. I decided to carry on looking into it and to meet with Martin again.'

John was shaking his head. 'What the hell were you thinking?' he said. 'Did you think about your career at any point? Or about our relationship?'

'I think I'd better just tell you everything,' she said, 'and then you can have a go at me, finish with me or whatever you have to do. I met Martin in a pub. This was last Friday. He told me that the person who gave him an alibi for the night of Phoebe's death was Nick, that same Nick who had stalked me.'

'What?' John leant forward towards her and his eyes widened; he brought his hand up to shield his eyes from the rays of the sun and then turned so his back was against the wall.

'I told you about Nick, didn't I?' she said.

'Yeah. I didn't make the connection.'

'Why would you? Well, he frequents that pub, so I wanted to get out of there and we went to Martin's flat.' She could see now that John looked tired. 'Whilst we were there, I had a couple of glasses of cider and eventually he told me what happened to Phoebe.' She took a deep breath. 'Martin was with her that night. He was very drunk and upset because she wouldn't take him back. He tried to jump over the balcony and Phoebe tried to stop him and lost her balance and fell.'

'Jesus!' said John. 'We didn't find any evidence he'd been there. I don't know what I can do with that information now.'

'Nothing, probably,' she said. 'You don't have to do anything, do you?'

John shrugged. 'There's no evidence, just hearsay.'

'No,' she said. 'I tried to record the conversations with Martin on my phone, but it didn't work.'

'Did he smash your phone?'

'Yes, but I don't think he knew I'd been trying to

record. There's something else I have to tell you.' She lowered her eyes for a moment, and then looked up at him. 'I let Martin kiss me.'

'Great,' he said; his voice was flat. He picked up his coffee and drank it, his eyes on her face. He put the cup down again. 'When you told me you'd stopped blaming yourself for Phoebe's death, this is why.'

'Yes.'

'You're happy to let Martin go free and not pay for causing her death, then, are you?'

'I'm not happy to,' she said, 'but he's quite vulnerable himself. He needs help really.'

'Oh, for Christ's sake! You're not thinking about trying to help him?'

'No, I can't help him, I know that. In fact, since finding out what happened, I'm seriously wondering if I want to carry on working as a therapist. If Phoebe hadn't come to me, she would still be alive.'

'You don't know that,' he said.

They both stood in silence. The voices and laughter from the tables outside the pub had grown louder. There were more people sitting at the tables, standing around with drinks and strolling along the river walk.

'I'm seeing Phoebe's mother on Saturday,' said Heather.

'What will you tell her?' said John.

'I'm still thinking about that,' she said. 'Her partner Alan throws his weight around a bit. Did I tell you about him? No. Anyway, I've arranged to see her on her own.'

'Well, be careful,' he said. 'Will it make things easier for her to hear that version, what you've just told me? Hey, you're a therapist. I'm sure you can make that call.'

She looked at him. Was that an endorsement of sorts? His face gave nothing away.

He looked at his watch. 'I've got to get back to work,' he said. 'Look, don't give up the day job. I'm sure you're great at it. Be thankful you've still got it.'

He touched her arm and walked away. He usually said he would call her, but he didn't say that, and he didn't look back.

25

On Saturday, Heather took a train to Farnham and a taxi from the station to Jean's house. She arrived late morning. As she stood outside the front door, she recalled her previous visits, after Phoebe's funeral and when she had hired a car a couple of weeks later. Both seemed an age ago; actually, eight months had passed since the funeral. As last time, she saw Jean through the frosted glass of the door. Jean opened the door, and Heather was struck by how much older she looked; her face was thinner, and she had dark rings under her eyes. She wore a scoop-neck black T-shirt and jeans and looked as if she had lost weight.

'Come in,' said Jean. 'I've been waiting for you. I'll make coffee.'

She showed Heather into the lounge and Heather sat again on the dark-blue sofa, opposite the sideboard topped with framed photographs of Phoebe as a baby and a schoolgirl. Her stomach churned as she prepared to tell Jean what she knew. She fidgeted with her phone and her bag, putting both down next to her as Jean came in with mugs of coffee on a tray. Jean handed her a mug, placed a plate of chocolate digestives on the tiled coffee table and sat in an armchair, as she had when Heather had visited before.

'Thank you for coming,' said Jean. 'You said you had something to tell me.'

'Yes,' said Heather. She put her coffee on the table. 'I know that Phoebe's death and the inquest and the lack of answers about what happened have been devastating for you. I'm mindful, though, that whilst we might want to know the truth, the truth can sometimes be difficult to hear.' Heather paused and clasped her hands together on her lap. 'Once you've heard something, you can't unhear it. I'm concerned about that, Jean.'

Jean sighed. 'Look, I have no peace the way things are. I go over and over various scenarios, constantly, about what might have happened. They're all horrific, nightmarish, but do you know what the worst one is?'

Heather shook her head. 'What is the worst one?'

Jean swallowed and looked close to tears. 'I see Phoebe, in despair and alone, drinking, because I know she drank a lot sometimes, and she just can't face living anymore. She thinks about calling me, perhaps, but she doesn't call me, because we weren't close – in fact, you could say we were estranged – and anyway, she wouldn't expect me to understand or be able to help her, so she goes onto the balcony and looks over and thinks, *it would be so easy, and all this would go away*, and she climbs over the railing and lets go and... she's gone. So if you're going to tell me that's what happened...' She smiled a sad smile. 'I was going to say, if that's what you were going to tell me, I'd rather you left now. But if you left, then I'd know, wouldn't I? So just tell me, please.'

'That's not what happened, Jean.'

Jean closed her eyes for a moment and let out another sigh. 'Thank you,' she said. 'I'm already sitting down, so go ahead.'

'You know Phoebe had a boyfriend called Martin, don't you?'

'Yes,' said Jean. 'Alan's convinced he had something to do with it. Go on.'

'She'd ended the relationship, but Martin couldn't accept that it was over. He kept going round to see her and she sometimes let him in. I think she felt sorry for him.'

Jean was nodding, her eyes fixed on Heather's face.

'That evening,' said Heather, 'he went round to Phoebe's flat, and he was very drunk. You have to remember that Martin was, and still is, very troubled and, at times, volatile.' She paused. 'He said he couldn't live without her and threatened to kill himself if she wouldn't take him back. She said again that they were finished. He went on to the balcony and started climbing over. Phoebe tried to stop him, and she helped him to get back onto the balcony, but in the process, she fell.'

Jean was immobile now, staring at her.

'So,' said Heather, 'Phoebe died saving Martin's life.'

They were both silent for a few minutes.

'How do you know this?' asked Jean.

'Martin told me, in the end.'

'It was his fault then,' said Jean.

'Yes.'

Jean screwed up her face, as if in physical pain. 'How come the police didn't find this out and charge him?'

'He had an alibi, a false alibi.'

'We must tell the police all this.'

'The police are aware,' said Heather. 'I know the detective in charge of the case, and I've told him what I found out. I thought it best to talk to him before meeting you. I'm not sure they can do anything now. They don't have any evidence.'

Heather picked up her coffee and took a sip; Jean did the same.

'I asked to see you on your own,' said Heather, 'and not with Alan, because I wanted you to know first and also, I didn't know how he would react. How do you think he'll take it?'

'He'll say I told you so and want to go and find Martin and... I don't know what. I can't deal with all that.'

They sat in silence. The sun streamed through the picture window, glinting on the glass in the photo frames on the sideboard so that the photographs were a blur of light.

'I'll tell Alan you were unable to find out anything more and I accept now that it was an accident, as the coroner said,' said Jean. 'Well, it was, wasn't it?'

'Will he go along with that?'

'He'll have to. If he wants us to keep seeing each other. It's enough to know what happened for me. I just want some peace.' Jean covered her face with her hands. When she removed them, her face was wet with tears. 'I have to tell my mother,' she said. 'I don't know what to tell her. She's very frail and confused now. She may have to go into a care home.'

'Does she talk about Phoebe?'

'Oh, yes. Phoebe was the apple of her eye. She sometimes talks about her as if she was still alive.'

'Do you need to tell her anything, then?' said Heather.

Heather hardly noticed a thing outside the taxi window on the way back to the station; she felt she was enclosed in a capsule of grief. She climbed on to the train, found a window seat and was relieved that no-one sat on the seat next to her, or on the two facing seats.

Jean had embraced her, as she was leaving, and had held on for some moments, and thanked her again. She had wished Jean well. She hoped Alan would accept what Jean had decided to tell him and that he would be a comfort to her. Clearly, he wanted the relationship to work, so perhaps he would cooperate. She hoped Phoebe's grandmother would be allowed whatever vagueness was needed to make her life bearable.

She was relieved that she'd visited Jean and that the visit was over. She hoped she'd handled it all right and had done no harm.

On Wednesday, Heather decided to go to Caffè Nero for lunch; lately, she'd resumed her habit of going there once a week. She hadn't heard from John and had resisted the temptation to call him.

The waitress brought her tuna panini, and she was just about to take a bite when Nick slid into the seat opposite her. She hadn't seen him come in. He had that strange smile on his face and his pale-blue eyes were cold and unblinking.

'I know about you and Martin,' he said.

Heather felt her face flush bright red. She put down the panini and wiped her fingers on a serviette.

'What are you talking about?' she said.

'Hah!' he said. 'It's no good playing the innocent. I

know you got off with Martin. He told me. Heather is an unusual name. I knew it was you.'

He tried to catch the waitress's eye, but she ignored him and continued to clear tables. He made a surly face at her back and started to get up.

'Young Martin is quite smitten with you,' he said. 'He's in a right state. Wait there. I'll be back.'

He went to the counter. Heather wanted to leave, but she remained seated, as if paralysed.

Nick returned with a small cappuccino. He leant towards her across the table.

'You and Martin!' he said.

'There is no me and Martin,' she said.

'You're lying.'

Heather felt a surge of irritation. After all she'd been through in the last few months, and after that stressful, painful meeting with Jean at the weekend, this was the last thing she needed.

'So, you told Martin I'd been your therapist, did you?' she said.

'Too right,' he said. 'He was interested in that. Really interested.' His smile had become a full-blown smirk. 'I wasn't going to make a complaint about you,' he said, 'but now I think I should seriously consider it. I have a lot to put in it, don't I?'

It was Heather's turn to lean across the table towards him. 'Martin asked you to give him an alibi for a certain evening last July, didn't he?'

'So?' he said.

'So, I believe there are severe penalties for telling lies to the police,' she said. She wrapped her panini in a serviette and picked up her bag. 'Giving a false alibi is lying, Nick.' She took a swig of her coffee and got up to leave.

Nick's pale-blue eyes looked colder than ever, and his smile had been wiped away.

Heather tried to phone John when she returned to the centre, but he was busy. Later that afternoon, she reached him. She told him Nick had reappeared, and about his threat and her own parting shot.

John called her on Friday and said he wanted to come round and give her an update. She was relieved to hear from him, and curious, as it sounded as if he had done something or had some news.

He came round early evening, as arranged, and when she saw his car draw up outside the house, she had a wistful sense of déjà vu. She switched the kettle on and went to the front door.

He had a growth of stubble, and his eyes looked tired. He made no move to kiss her. They went into the lounge, and he sat on the settee. Heather fetched mugs of coffee and sat in her usual armchair.

'How did it go with Phoebe's mother?' he asked.

'It was very painful,' she said, 'very sad. Jean's been haunted by the idea that Phoebe might have taken her own life, and what I told her was easier to bear than that, I think. Well, I'm sure it was.'

John nodded and reached for his mug of coffee.

'One good thing is, Jean said she wouldn't tell Alan,' she said. 'She'll tell him she accepts that it was an accident. I'm relieved about that. And she was thinking about what to tell her own mother; she may not tell her anything, as the grandmother is confused and sometimes thinks Phoebe is still alive.'

'OK,' said John. 'That sounds... as good as can be expected.'

Birds were singing, and through the window at the far end of the room, Heather could see birds flitting about in the branches of the trees in the back garden. She looked at John again. How familiar his face was, and yet there was this strange new distance between them.

'You wanted to give me an update,' she said.

'Yeah,' he said. 'After what you told me, we picked up Nick Wheeler.'

'Right,' she said. She felt a rush of nervous excitement.

'Your friend Martin told Nick he got off with you and it seems Nick was jealous,' he said.

'I didn't exactly get off with Martin.'

'Well, anyway...' said John. He closed his eyes for a few seconds and then said, 'He admitted his alibi was false and withdrew it.'

'Really? That is a result.'

Heather was cringing inside and at the same time, she had a sense of jubilation.

'He's a nasty piece of work,' said John. 'Malicious, no moral compass, lack of affect – is that what you say? Psychopathic tendencies, perhaps.'

'Did he say why he gave Martin the alibi?'

John shrugged. 'He wanted to be liked, I guess. He said Martin was a mate who wanted a favour. Maybe he thought he could hold it over him somehow; I wouldn't be surprised. Anyway, I advised him that he could be charged with wasting police time, or even perverting the course of justice, and informed him of the possible penalties. It put the wind up him, I can assure you.'

'Will you charge him?'

'That depends. It came up that he'd been thinking of making a complaint about you. I advised him against doing that.' John raised his eyebrows and smiled a weary smile.

'Thank you,' said Heather, and she tried to smile back. 'You've probably saved my skin.'

'Yep, I probably have.'

'What about Martin?' she asked. 'Will you do anything?'

'He's pathetic,' said John. 'I might have a word with him.'

Heather was surprised to feel a sharp pang of guilt about Martin, as if he were a child she'd been responsible for and had abandoned.

'Poor Martin,' she said.

'Don't waste your sympathy on him,' said John, sharply.

Heather remembered thinking, long ago, that she wouldn't want to be on the wrong side of him. She hoped she wasn't now.

'I have to go,' he said, and got up from the settee.

She followed him into the hall.

'Is that it for us?' she said.

He was looking down at the floor, and then he raised his head and faced her.

'I need some time,' he said. 'Just give me some time.' He laid his hand on her arm and his touch sent an electric shock through her body, just as it had that day when he was leaving the café, after they'd met, in the beginning, to talk about Phoebe. He'd left his biro on the table; she still had it in her bag.

She went to the kitchen before her supervision and Val was there, waiting for the kettle to boil. Heather was relieved to see her smiling, lived-in face and kind brown eyes. Val wore her trademark loose top and baggy linen trousers. She'd brought in some liquorice teabags and persuaded Heather to try one. They made their way to the consulting room, with mugs of spicy tea.

Heather began by telling Val that Nick had reappeared and threatened to make a complaint against her. She told her that she knew a police officer and had told him and thought Nick would leave her alone now.

Val raised her eyebrows and leant forward as if she wanted to say something, and then she stopped herself.

After pausing for a moment, she said, 'How do you feel about that?'

'It shook me,' said Heather. 'Also, there have been developments regarding my client, Phoebe, who died last year. I'd like to tell you about that.'

Val nodded. 'Yes, please tell me,' she said.

Heather told Val that she'd found out what happened to Phoebe, and explained how her death had been caused by the reckless behaviour of her ex-boyfriend. She was grateful Val didn't ask how she knew.

'That's really shocking,' said Val, 'and so sad.'

'I've told the police,' said Heather. 'I don't know whether they'll do anything. I know now that I wasn't to blame. I didn't miss something, and I couldn't have prevented it.' She paused and took a breath. 'I know all that on one level, but still, I can't shake off the feeling that I have done terrible harm. And I've been wondering whether I want to continue to work as a therapist.'

'Goodness,' said Val. 'Let's unpack this. I can understand why you might feel that way. What happened to Phoebe is very disturbing. And there was the inquest. Oh, and there's also this business with the obsessed young man, Nick. You've had such a difficult time recently. You must be emotionally drained.'

'Yes, it's all that, and more,' said Heather.

She went on to tell Val about David and how he blamed her, and therapy, for the difficulties in his marriage.

'Hmm,' said Val. 'It's true there can be unintended consequences when things change and people change. It's also true that therapists can do harm and can even ruin people's lives. But you have not. You've done a lot of good work. Now, I'm aware of the irony in what I'm about to say, because you're having a crisis of confidence in psychotherapy, but how would you feel about going back into therapy yourself? You're not seeing anyone at present, are you?'

Heather shook her head.

'Think about it,' said Val. 'It would give you space for yourself, to work through these doubts and anxieties. They are perfectly natural, given all that's happened. If, after some time talking to someone, you still want to leave your job and change direction, fair enough. But please, don't make any hasty decisions, will you?'

'All right,' said Heather. 'That could be helpful.'

'Are you due any leave? It could be good to get away.'

'Yes, I might do that,' said Heather. She wanted to visit her father. And she longed to see Max, to be able to talk to him, in person, not over the phone, and to see the stone buildings of Stirling again, to walk up to the castle with him and breathe the clean air. She would call him; she had a lot to tell him.

'Try the tea,' said Val, and she picked up her mug. 'It's very comforting. By the way, each teabag has a little motto.' She took hold of a square tag on the end of the string hanging over the rim of the mug and squinted at it. 'Mine says: *People who love are giving.* Oh well, some of them are more inspiring.'

Heather grasped the soggy tag attached to her teabag and read out the motto: '*If you help somebody, you awaken them.*'

Val clapped her hands together and laughed. 'There you are,' she said. 'It's serendipity. The universe sent you that. My work is done!'

Heather couldn't help smiling. 'Shall I tell you about my other clients?' she said.

This book is printed on paper from sustainable sources managed under the Forest Stewardship Council (FSC) scheme.

It has been printed in the UK to reduce transportation miles and their impact upon the environment.

For every new title that Troubador publishes, we plant a tree to offset CO_2, partnering with the More Trees scheme.

MORE TREES
LET'S PLANT A BILLION TREES

For more about how Troubador offsets its environmental impact, see www.troubador.co.uk/sustainability-and-community